Carolrhoda Lab™ is a trademark of Lerner Publishing Group, Inc.

Carolrhoda Lab™
An imprint of Carolrhoda Books
A division of Lerner Publishing Group, Inc.
241 First Avenue North
Minneapolis, MN 55401 U.S.A.

Website address: www.lernerbooks.com

Main body text set in Helvetica Neue 10.5/15.
Typeface provided by Adobe Systems.

Library of Congress Cataloging-in-Publication Data

Nelson, Vaunda Micheaux.
    No crystal stair / by Vaunda Micheaux Nelson ; illustrated by R. Gregory
Christie.
        p.   cm.
    ISBN: 978-0-7613-6169-5 (trade hard cover : alk. paper)
    ISBN: 978-0-7613-8727-5 (eBook)
    1. Michaux, Lewis H., 1885?-1976—Juvenile fiction. 2. Bookstores—New
York (State)—New York—Juvenile fiction. 3. African Americans—Books
and reading—Juvenile fiction. 4. Harlem (New York, N.Y.)—Juvenile fiction.
I. Christie, R. Gregory, 1971– ill. II. Title.
PZ7.N43773N6 2012
[Fic]—dc23   2011021251

Manufactured in the United States of America
3 – PP – 4/1/13

NO CRYSTAL STAIR

A DOCUMENTARY NOVEL
OF THE LIFE AND WORK OF
LEWIS MICHAUX, HARLEM BOOKSELLER

VAUNDA MICHEAUX NELSON
ARTWORK BY R. GREGORY CHRISTIE

🌿 carolrhoda LAB
MINNEAPOLIS

TO UNCLE LONNIE AND HIS VISION

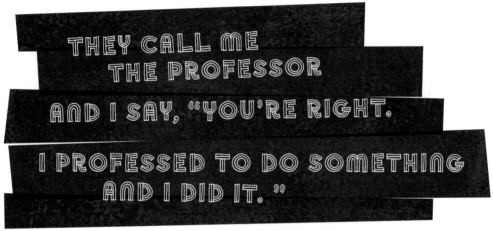

THEY CALL ME
THE PROFESSOR

AND I SAY, "YOU'RE RIGHT.

I PROFESSED TO DO SOMETHING
AND I DID IT."

—LEWIS MICHAUX

SECTION 1
1906–1922

PICKING PIGS

1906

LEWIS

Everybody keeps saying be satisfied with Jesus's love, and he will give us our daily bread. I keep waiting, but we never get any bread, so I have to go out and do things for myself.

When I asked Poppa for a bicycle, he said, "Pray, son, and the Lord will provide."

I prayed a whole year, but even Santa Claus didn't bring me a bicycle.

When I asked Poppa about it, he said, "Don't rush the Lord. The Lord will act in due time."

I went to find Mother to see what she had to say. She was in the kitchen baking shortening bread and singing, "   lp if you take the first step."

I said, "Mother, I never heard you sing that hymn before."

"That's not a hymn, son, that's a prayer," she explained. "You see me washing dishes, sweeping the floor, putting a patch on your daddy's pants. When I sing that, it's my prayer. God is helping me because I'm making an effort."

I went outside and walked down the road near our house thinking about what she said. There was a boy riding a bicycle. The boy got off, leaned the bicycle against a tree, and went to picking berries. I thought I'd follow Mother's prayer and "take the first step." I "stepped" on that bicycle and started off down the road.

Ha! I looked back and there wasn't nobody coming after me, so I said, "Thank you, Jesus."

Mother's prayer worked.

JOHN HENRY MICHAUX

Lewis isn't a bad boy. He does his part in the store. But now he's been missing school, and I can't do nothing with him. Some of my customers been calling him a "smart Negro," and they're not referring to his intelligence. He *is* intelligent, just headstrong. Willful.

I've not always been there for my children. I spent most of my time building my business. Started off as a merchant seaman, then after I married Blanche, took to peddling fish in Newport News. We were starting a family and I needed to settle down. Near broke my back, but I managed to save enough money to open my own seafood and produce store right here on Jefferson Avenue. Had to do some dealings with white merchants that might be called compromising. Some of my cronies called me Uncle Tom for what I put up with. I got the last laugh—my own store and a bar and a restaurant too. We're doing just fine.

Except Lewis . . . he needs more attention than I been giving. When you got nine children, it's not easy to keep track. One of them's bound to stray.

Blanche did teach Lewis his Bible. Matter of fact, without her, I wouldn't have much religion myself. Became a Baptist because of her.

Blanche is a good wife and I love her, but she's got her faults. Doted on our boy Lightfoot from the day he was born with that blasted caul over his face. Said it meant he was destined to some high mission. I tell her it's wrong for a parent to favor any child, but Blanche can't help herself. She tries with Lewis, but he sees how she is with his brother.

Blanche is strung tight as a banjo. Doctors say it's a nervous condition, and dealing with the day-to-day keeping of the house takes its toll. She don't have a whole lot of fortitude. Lord knows we have enough children, but she never got over the four we lost.

She's right about Lightfoot, though. He's special, and he knows what he's about. Lewis is searching. He has to find his way, like a sailor who drops anchor in many ports before he finds a dock that feels right, a place of belonging.

I believe Lewis and I come from the same soil. When I'm discussing my ideas about the need for our race to be self-sufficient, his eyes never leave my face. The other day I heard him talking with other Negro boys about standing up for themselves.

He said, "You gotta do for yourself, 'cause nobody's gonna do for you."

Made me proud. The way that boy thinks, I have to remind myself he's only nine years old.

BLANCHE MICHAUX

When I first met John Henry, he was a simple man, full of dreams. I loved to hear his sea stories and his plans for making something of himself. And he wasn't just trying to impress me. He meant what he said. He's a respected businessman now and a good provider. All he needed was some religion, and praise God, he finally got on board that train.

But Henry lives at the store. Even after closing, he finds something that needs doing or he's meeting with some highfalutin politician or such. He doesn't have time to take me out like when we were courting. Seems like all I ever do is make babies and pick up after people.

Mama warned me about marrying a light-skinned man with straight hair and ambition. Said people'd see me as less than him because I'm not pretty. She sure was right about that. Most days, I find myself feeling lonely.

Thank the Lord for Lightfoot Solomon—the joy of my life. Henry expects Lightfoot'll take over the store after he's gone, but I keep telling Henry the Lord has bigger plans for our son, *much* bigger plans.

Lewis is still just a boy, but we could school him to take over when Henry retires. He's a sharp one, sometimes too clever for his own good. He might see the respectable path if he wasn't so busy getting himself into trouble. Henry seems to expect me to straighten him out, but that's a father's job. I've spent many a sleepless night lying in bed thinking about Lewis, trying to figure him out. I guess it must be hard living in the shadow of an older brother who was born for greatness. Stealing may just be his way of saying, "Look at me!"

I try. I do. But I'm tired. And sometimes I feel like the room I'm in just keeps getting smaller, so small I can hardly breathe.

LEWIS

When I get home today, I hear Ruthie crying like her world is ending. Nobody seems to be paying her any mind, so I go to Ruth's crib to check on her. I can tell she's been at it for a while. She's all red in the face and stinking like she's messed herself. I try to make her stop bawling but can't, and Mother's just sitting at the kitchen table staring out the window.

"Ruth's having a fit in there, Mother."

She doesn't answer.

"Mother," I say, "Ruth . . ."

"I hear her" is all she says. She says it real quiet like. Doesn't even look at me.

I run back to Ruth and pat her on the head. Whew, she smells so bad I don't want to pick her up. But she's screaming now and I want her to stop. I wonder where my brothers and sisters are.

"Mother, please!"

She doesn't come. I'm getting a clean diaper when Poppa comes home.

"Go on now," he says, "I'll do this."

I go outside and cover my ears until, finally, Ruthie stops crying. Then *I* start crying.

BLANCHE

I need a little quiet. Just one hour. I give Courtney some money from the tin I keep behind the sugar and have her take Julius, Norris, Margaret, Benny and Jennie to get ice cream. I tell her to take them for a walk after. A good long walk. Then I sit myself down with a nice cup of hot coffee.

One hour is all I'm asking. One hour.

I get fifteen minutes. Fifteen minutes before Ruth starts. I know I should go to her. Her diaper likely needs changing. But I can't make myself move.

It won't hurt Ruth to cry a while. Too much holding will spoil a child.

Thank God, Lewis gets home. Lord knows where that boy's been or what he's been up to, but right now, I'm just glad he's here. He can tend Ruth. One hour's all I'm asking.

When John Henry comes, he touches my hand with a tenderness I haven't felt in a long time.

"You need to rest awhile," he says, helping me to stand. "Don't worry about supper."

In my mind I'm shouting, thank you, thank you, thank you, Henry, but I don't think I'm saying it out loud. I'm concentrating on getting my feet to move. I'd run if I could.

Finally, I'm in bed. It feels good to lie down. So good. Henry touches my face, then leaves me. It's quiet. Quiet. Thank the Lord for a little quiet.

Intake Clerk

CENTRAL STATE HOSPITAL, PETERSBURG, VIRGINIA

Well, we got another crier, that new patient, Blanche Michaux. Of course, the doctors are calling it "Nervous Exhaustion." I just write down what they tell me.

She's exhausted, all right, nervous, too, but in the old days, back when this place was the Central Lunatic Asylum, we called it "hysteria." Now they're trying to be nicer so people won't feel shamed by being here. You get reprimanded for the word "crazy," but it seems to me that about says it.

I do feel sorry for Mrs. Michaux, though. All them kids. Ten or eleven, I hear. She's like that old nursery rhyme, the old woman in the shoe. I tell you, these men. They get us pregnant, then go on back to work, and we don't see them again until dinnertime (if we're lucky), or the next time they want some honey.

When he brought her in, he said, "She just keeps crying or sleeping." I wanted to say, well, mister, when was the last time you fixed her dinner or took her out dancing? That's what I want to know. Sometimes women like her are just lonely.

Maybe Mrs. Michaux will be one of them that snaps out of it pretty quick. Some do. A few months in here and they're okay. Just need some rest is all. She was crying when she came in, but she kept telling her husband things to remember about taking care of the children. Must love them. Patients do better if they have a reason to get back home.

LIGHTFOOT SOLOMON MICHAUX

Things haven't been the same since Mother got home from that mental institution. Poppa treats her like a child, and they say things to each other that a man and wife shouldn't. I made the mistake of telling Poppa I think he should be more patient with her. He told me, in no uncertain terms, to mind my own business.

All I can do is pray on it. She's in God's hands. And Poppa has a heavy burden to bear. He's an important man, superior to most. Men like him need some leeway, especially from the family. He was right to chastise me.

I don't want conflict between us. There has been enough because of my marriage to Mary Eliza. Though he has not been disrespectful, Poppa certainly has not welcomed her with affection. I am keeping faith that time will enable him to accept her as my wife and his daughter-in-law. Mary is a formidable woman, opinionated, too, which may make winning Poppa over a challenge. He prefers a woman who is content to remain in her husband's shadow. Lord knows, Mary can be a handful, but she is surely good for me—strong, industrious, diligent, and frugal. She will serve us well in our business and whatever the future brings.

Lewis doesn't help. Telling me and everyone who cares to listen that I chose Mary because of her light skin. And Poppa, for reasons I don't understand, encourages him. There is something between Lewis and Poppa that runs deep.

LEWIS

I tried to make some money picking berries. That farmer man was paying two cents a quart, and the best you could pick was ten quarts a day. Twenty cents worth.

There were about a hundred kids picking. That fat white man, with his great big hat on, set up under a willow tree with crates and boxes all around. We'd bring him a quart of berries, and he'd give us a two-cent coin. Them old-timey, two-cent copper coins are so big, when we get ten, we think we're rich.

Then one day last week after I picked about a half a quart of berries, I stopped and looked at this man's place. He had corn, tomatoes, cabbage—all kinds of vegetables. He had cows, sheep, mules, horses, chickens, pigs, and I don't know what all else. And I wondered, how did this man get all this? Picking berries? No, he got it stealing. Stealing the sweat of colored boys like me.

So I took that half quart of berries and ate them. Then I went down to his barn. There were lots of sacks filled with corn. I tried to pick one up, but it was too heavy, so I emptied one of those croaker sacks and took it over to the pigpen. The sows had some itty-bitty babies, and I went over there and took three of them and put them in the bag. Then I went down the road to a water tank and sat there until a freight train stopped to fill up. I got on. Didn't know where it was going, but I needed to get away with those squealers.

Sometime down the road the train stopped and I hopped off. I tied those pigs to a tree and looked around. Down through the woods I saw a lumber mill where some colored men were hauling logs. I went down there and said to one of the men, "You want to buy a pig?"

He said, "Pig? Where you going to get a pig?"

I said, "I ain't got to get the pig. Already got the pig."

So he comes back through the woods with me, and I sold those three pigs for $1.50 each. I made $4.50 in two hours. Now I'm in business. I'm not picking berries no more. I'm picking pigs.

JOHN HENRY

The judge sentenced my boy to twenty lashes for stealing a sack of peanuts. A sack of peanuts! Lewis needed to be punished, but this was harsh. The police whipped him behind the courthouse. And all I could do was stand there and watch them beat my boy.

They expect he'll learn from this treatment. He will, but not what they think. Lewis didn't cry out. Only fourteen years old and didn't cry out . . . refused to. Just glared straight ahead . . . angry. The boy is stubborn. Keeps right on taking things. I've been trying to reach him, send him down a better path than the one he's on. But he's gotten worse since Blanche came home from the hospital.

Been stealing livestock from some of our neighbors—white ones, so it makes things worse for the boy. And that doesn't do me—or my business—any good. I get produce from some of these folks.

1915

LIGHTFOOT

Poppa makes excuses for him, but I know he is shamed by Lewis's shenanigans. I remember back in the day when Lewis and I worked together pushing Poppa's fish cart down Jefferson Avenue. Lewis was nine or ten, I guess. He'd yell

Clams and Oysters worth a holler!
Step right up and bring them dollars!
Best in town, I couldn't be prouder!
If you don't buy, I'll say it louder!

Then he'd start it over, louder. People would laugh but then come over and buy fish. Lewis is surely clever, and people like him.

Now he's nineteen years old and serving time. I pray for him. Maybe that chain gang will straighten him out.

LEWIS

When I got locked up, the old judge says to me, "Boy, what do you do to live?"

I say, "I do like the white folks."

"And what is that?"

I say, "Breathe. What else could you do to live?"

He says, "You being smart, boy?"

I say, "I don't mean it that way. This is the way you asked it, 'What you do to live?' I say to live, I breathe."

He says, "I mean, what do you do for a living?"

I say, "You got me locked up for what I do. The same thing white folks do."

He says, "What is that?"

I say, "Steal. You came to America and stole America from the Indians. Then that was so good, you went to Africa and stole my ancestors and enslaved us."

The judge didn't answer. Just sentenced me.

LEWIS

You can't walk straight on a crooked line. You try, you'll break your leg. How can you walk straight in a crooked system? Even Poppa knows that.

He was always saying how he had more brands of whiskey than anybody ever thought of, and I found out why. One day—I wasn't more than nine years old—Poppa sent Lightfoot and me down to the cellar to get some bottles of Old Sod and Old Henry for the bar. Poppa had twenty-three bottles with different labels on them. But there was only one barrel of whiskey down there. Just one. He put the same whiskey in the Old Sod bottle, the same whiskey in the Old Henry bottle, and the same whiskey in every other bottle. Customers would come in and say, "Gimme a shot of that Old Turkey this time. It's smoother than Old Sod." They didn't even know the difference. Well, that taught me something. Taught me that people don't know half the things they need to know.

Make no mistake. Poppa works and hard. Nothing was handed to him. It's true he had to do some kowtowing to get his business going. I remember hearing him "SIR"ing them while they were "BOY"ing him and worse behind his back. They would charge Poppa more for stock than white merchants, like he was just some dumb Negro who didn't know. Well, he wasn't so dumb. Poppa knew. And while they weren't looking, Poppa became the self-sufficient black man Marcus Garvey talks about.

Marcus Garvey, 1919

A fellow told me the other day, "It don't make no difference. Your daddy's still working for the white man."

I said, "Well, maybe so, but not directly. And that's something."

When I look at Poppa, I see him bent over with all kinds of ailments. I'll never break myself up working for the white man. I'm going to use my head and stay off my knees.

JOHN HENRY

Been reading Marcus Garvey's newspaper the *Negro World*, and I'm hopeful about what he is saying. I know his talk of separate communities for blacks isn't popular, but maybe we need to find *ourselves* before we can find our true place in the white world. I needed to work with whites . . . needed to accept tradeoffs that I'm not proud of. It was that or work *for* somebody else . . . never build anything of my own. Our people had enough of that in slavery.

Garvey is saying what I believed all along. We need to take pride in our race, embrace our history. We need more black institutions under black leadership. Like Tuskegee. Like my store. I'm proud of that.

Lewis is a believer. We're kindreds all right. Some evenings we spend hours talking about one of Garvey's articles or sharing ideas about race. Lewis has passion. There's hope for him.

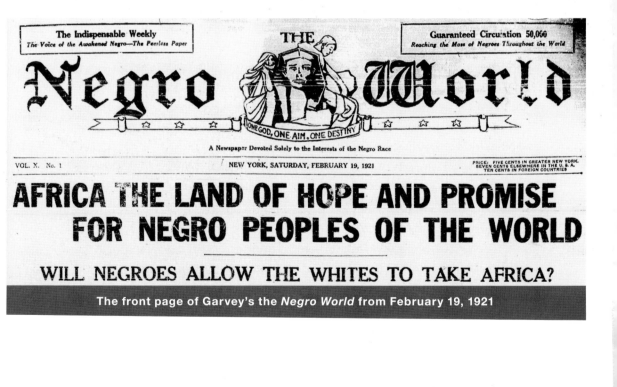

The front page of Garvey's the *Negro World* from February 19, 1921

LEWIS

Garvey's right. "A race without authority and power is a race without respect." We're not going to gain power by holding out our hands to the white man, waiting for him to give us something. We gotta take it. We have to create our *own* opportunities.

Most folks don't get Garvey's idea with the Black Star Line. People say, "I don't want to go back to Africa. I'm an American." But what Garvey's trying to create is a connection between people of African ancestry all over the world, between displaced Africans—not just in the United States but everywhere—and the Mother Africa. We need to know and support each other because it's clear that white America doesn't want integration. Never will. We're deceiving ourselves if we think we'll ever be accepted. So, like Garvey says, we need to unite and take care of our own.

Garvey's *Negro World* has been a gift. It started Poppa and me talking. We've shared more in the past six months than all our years put together. I wish we'd gotten here sooner.

Poppa's life is over. Anyone can see he's not well. I know what's coming.

JOHN HENRY

I suppose my business will die with me. I don't know where Lewis will end up, but his heart isn't in the store. It looked for a while like Lightfoot would take over. He's been working by my side all these years. Did a good job getting those military contracts. Feeding all those soldiers down at Camp Lee has been good business, both financially and politically. It can't hurt to have government connections.

He'd never admit it, but Lightfoot is just like Lewis. Stubborn. He wants something of his own. Seems he's looking to find it in the church, especially since he met Mary. She's like Blanche when it comes to religion, only more so. Makes sense though. Lightfoot's the only one of my boys who doesn't smoke, doesn't drink. And he'll give you a sermon about it anytime you want, but mostly when you *don't.* Not much money in church work, but like Blanche says, Lightfoot may be destined for something higher.

I thought Norris might take an interest in the store, but I can't get him out of the pool hall long enough to find out. He has gambling in his blood and seems more a follower than a leader. Right now he's following his older brother Lewis, and that path is a rocky one.

But I can't be worrying on it. I've done what I can and I'm tired.

LIGHTFOOT

Poppa worked hard and I know he wanted someone to assume his role, but the store is holding me back. My Church of God is growing, and the Lord doesn't want a part-time employee.

Lewis was doing well in the business. I know he's felt undervalued. I had hoped that being put in charge might help Lewis find his worth. He deceived me for a while. I was beginning to think he had changed his ways. I was trusting him. But then *this* stunt, right after Poppa's funeral. Taking off with a thousand dollars.

I hear he's in Philadelphia running a gambling house. Doesn't he know he's partnered with the Devil?

NORRIS MICHAUX

Lewis has the right idea. Newport News is an ain't-goin'-nowhere town. If I stay here, Lightfoot will try to talk me into running the store. That's not me. Poppa knew it. I don't want it and he wouldn't want me in it.

I'm taking the train to Philly. Maybe I can get in on some of Lewis's action. Pool's my game, but I'll sit in on poker or craps or whatever's on the table.

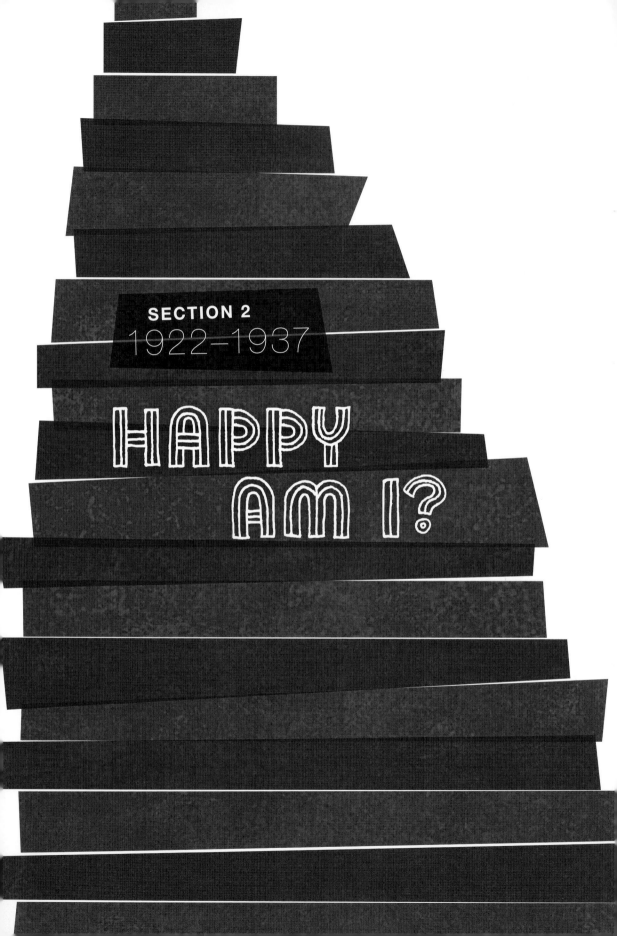

HAPPY
AM I?

LEWIS

I took some store money. So what? I earned it. Worked my bee-hind off for it. Poppa would understand. I needed to get out of that town.

Is it my fault the store's closing? Lightfoot's doing *his* thing. I say, fine, let me do mine. Papa said build something of your own. Lightfoot's using store money for that church of his. I'm building my own something too.

Lightfoot said, "If you needed money, why didn't you just ask?"

I laughed. He knew why. If I *had* asked for the money, all he'd've given me was a sermon.

Lightfoot is on my back too because Norris followed me up here. But Norris is a full-grown man, making his own choices. In fact, he's developed quite a reputation for himself. He's a shark at the pool table. And people've nicknamed him Charleston because he's a real heel-kicker on the dance floor.

I'm doing a good business here. Been putting the cut box on the table, and on Monday morning it's full of nickels and dimes. I don't do like some other people who gamble do—go downtown with fancy women and big shots and then have blue Monday. I dump that box of house winnings on the table and say, "You all are going to win this money back." And every time I open the door, the house is full.

Some of my regular customers are "upstanding citizens." Would be a problem for them if their Sunday-go-to-meetin' folks knew. But nobody'll hear it from me. I tell my customers, "Discreet is my middle name." They just laugh and put more money on the table.

I have to watch myself though. One night last week, I had too many shots of whiskey and things got rowdy. The police came down here on a raid and I ended up in court. Old Judge Fisher sentenced me to six months. When court was over, they put me in a paddy wagon to carry me to the workhouse. About two blocks from the workhouse, we stopped, the driver came back, unlocked the wagon, and said, "You get lost." I got lost and came on back and was open for business the next day. Looks like I have "upstanding" friends in high places.

LEWIS

OCTOBER 16 I know I shouldn't be laughing, but I can't help myself. My perfect brother went and got himself thrown in jail for singing in the street. Ha! Ha! Ha! Now I'm not the only one in the family with a police record.

Some people in Newport News complained about the music from one of his outdoor church programs. He and his congregation were marching through the streets singing hymns. I guess his voice was so bad they charged him with disturbing the peace.

I wonder if my brother was humiliated or if he did it to get the attention. Whichever, he handled it. Handled it just fine. Lightfoot defended himself and soaked the courtroom in so much Scripture he got acquitted. Amen.

NEGRO PREACHER AND CONGREGATION THROWN INTO POLICE LOCKUP

Despite a warning from the court on Thursday, the Rev. Lightfoot Michaux and members of his Church of God again marched through a sleeping East End neighborhood singing hymns at 4:00 A.M. yesterday. This time, the preacher paid the price. He and members of his congregation were arrested and placed in police lockup. Michaux was fined $22.50 on a disorderly charge.

Pointing to the fifty followers packed in the courtroom, Justice John B. Locke said, "Now as for these people, they simply followed you. I don't want to fine them. You are responsible."

"Yes," said the revivalist, "I and God."

Justice Locke shook his head and smiled. "Well, I'm not holding God responsible."

At Thursday's hearing, Justice Locke told Michaux, "This thing must stop."

"Well, sir," the revivalist replied, "if the Lord leads me out 25th Street at four o'clock tomorrow morning, we will go. It rests with God. If He leads us, we will follow Him."

Justice Locke turned to Police Chief C. M. Campbell and said, "Chief, if the Lord leads him through the East End tomorrow morning, let yourself be led to arrest Michaux and all those with him."

This is exactly what occurred.

For several weeks the preacher and his wife have been holding revival services at 35th Street and Chestnut Avenue. Nearly every morning they have marched out from Jefferson Avenue singing what the preacher called "songs of correction, to awaken sinners from their slumbers that they may meditate upon their transgressions." Annoyed residents complained to local police.

Philadelphia Police Officer

I didn't mean to put the punk's eye out. If he'da just done what I said, I wouldn'ta hit him. We threw these perps in the paddy wagon, and Michaux kept carpin' on somethin'. I told him, sit down and hush up, but he kept on. My nightstick closed his yap. I hate skels with no respect for the badge. My stick smashed the guy's glasses and popped his peeper. Not pretty. If he'da just kept his smart-ass trap shut.

I knew sooner or later there'd be trouble at that place. It's no secret Michaux was runnin' a card palace, but he was pretty good about payin' the pad. Michaux's got connections, but we can't let that kind of ruckus slide. When there's gunplay, we gotta move in. We got boundaries.

I hear his brother took a bullet over a craps game. Sounds like he'll be okay, but it cost Michaux that eye.

NORRIS

Man, that joker was out of control. Accuses me of cheating, then starts bangin' away like he's Wyatt Earp or something. Just got me through the side though. Guess it wasn't my time. But it was close, too close. When I felt the burn and saw all that blood, I thought my time was up.

Lightfoot says the Lord is telling me to change my ways. He might have a point. Maybe after I get out of this hospital, I'll lay low for a while. Sounds like Lewis will be closing up his place anyway. Maybe I should take my wife and pay a visit to her Pittsburgh relations. Sinah's been missing her family.

LEWIS

Sometimes it's a good idea to just keep quiet. When the cops raided us, they took Norris to the hospital in an ambulance and put me and some of my customers in a patrol wagon. One of my regulars was going on about how he might lose his job, and I was telling him to take it easy.

An officer said to me, "Sit over there before I heat you up." I thought he said, "before I *eat* you up."

I said to him, "Officer, if you eat me up, you will have more sense in your belly than you've got in your head." I was pretty tickled with myself until he turned around and clubbed me across my face with his nightstick.

The doctors are giving me a glass eye. Like I said, sometimes it's a good idea to just keep quiet.

I'm glad Norris is okay, even though he started this whole mess. I don't know if he threw snake eyes or not. He grabbed up the dice so fast I didn't really see. Said he didn't, but it wouldn't surprise me.

When that other fool pulled his piece, I was kicking myself for not making him leave earlier. He had that look, right on the edge of desperate. Maybe he owed somebody. Hindsight—it don't change things.

Could be worse though. Norris is alive, and so am I, even with one eye. And neither of us is going to jail. We can thank Lightfoot for that. Came to bail me out but, instead, sweet-talked that judge who released me into my preacher brother's custody. Lightfoot's been looking to save my soul for a long time, so I know he's enjoying this. I'm not complaining. Don't have nothing now, and I don't deny this soul could benefit from some attention.

The glass eye won't make a whole lot of difference. I've been half blind my whole life anyway.

LIGHTFOOT

May God's will be done. Surely now my brothers see the dangers of their sinful behavior. The Lord has given both new paths to walk. I think Norris will be fine. He has his wild side, but he also has a good wife and is building a family. Perhaps this brush with eternity will settle him down.

Lewis will need more guidance. And *now* is the time. Losing his eye and his "business" have made him penetrable, and I'm not sorry about that. I am not taking advantage of his vulnerability; the Lord has given me this opportunity. It is His desire that I direct Lewis to His service.

1927

LEWIS

Lightfoot got himself arrested again, but I'm not laughing this time. Sure, I rode him about it, but truth be told, it was a race issue. Lightfoot was baptizing whites and colored folks in the same service. The cops arrested him for holding an integrated baptism.

This sickens me. The Klan is pulling somebody's strings in Virginia government. Nobody can tell me the KKK isn't behind that new statute requiring racially separate seating in public places. Not only can't the church have integrated baptisms now, but coloreds and whites can't even sit together in the pews during services.

No wonder people don't know how to get along.

BLANCHE

If those judges would listen to what my son is saying, they would see the truth—that the laws of God rank higher than the laws of the State. Lightfoot told the judge that his calling is to preach the gospel to *every* creature. He said, "Virginia's ungodly segregation laws must stop at the threshold of God's House."

He was speaking to people without ears. Lightfoot paid the fine, but I know my son. His heart will not be changed. He will continue to welcome *all* people into his church. His greatness will not be challenged.

The fact that Lewis has returned home and found the Lord is proof of Lightfoot's sway.

LIGHTFOOT

My precious ones, the sermon tonight will be built around a great subject, or a question, rather. The text is found in Mark, the 12th chapter and the 23rd verse. A woman hath had three husbands. They all have died. Gone to Heaven. In Heaven, whose wife is she?

I see some of you sisters are getting very anxious!

But this text will not be preached until the collection hath been raised. Come forward my lambs with your offerings.

LEWIS

Mother always said Lightfoot would achieve great things. And he's proving her right. My brother *can* preach. I'll give him that. He knows money too. That's Poppa's legacy. I'm proud.

The Gospel Spreading Association is a good name for the business side of the ministry. The Church of God *is* spreading, that's for sure. Lightfoot's already got churches in Newport News, Hampton, Baltimore, Edenborn, and Washington, and is laying the groundwork for others in New York City and Philadelphia. He's preaching over the radio now too. Who'd have thought that first little tent service on Jefferson Avenue would lead to this?

It's not so bad being back in Newport News . . . for now. The church folks are treating me kindly, although there's some whispering about my "unholy" past. It's good to be with the family. And tomorrow I'm getting hitched. I wonder what my cronies in Philly would say if they could see me now.

It's no secret Lightfoot arranged this marriage . . . another move toward my salvation. I'm not complaining. Sister Willie is a fine, I mean, *fine-* looking woman. A good one too. I just hope she knows what she's getting.

WILLIE ANN ALLEN

Tomorrow Brother Lewis and I will be married before God. Elder Michaux desires this, and he surely knows better than I. Sister Michaux seems uncertain about our union, but I have prayed on it and am trusting in the Lord. Brother Lewis is intelligent, even charming at times, and treats me with respect. He has his shortcomings, but don't we all? Perfection can only be found in our Lord and Savior Jesus Christ. It is easier to do the right thing when that's all you've ever done. But when you've succumbed to temptation as Brother Lewis has, you have a steeper hill to climb.

Brother Lewis is not like other men in the Church. He needs a strong partner to help him move toward redemption. Is it my obligation to be that person? Perhaps I am part of a plan greater than myself, but is it a sin to marry one man when you love another?

Lewis and Willie Ann pose for a wedding portrait.

Dear Lord, I come before you to ask that you deliver me from these feelings that I have for the man who is not to be my husband. I pray that you give me the strength to be the wife you would have me be to Brother Lewis and ask that you lead me to understand my purpose and guide me in doing your will. I ask this in the holy name of my Lord and Savior Jesus Christ. Amen.

Church of God Official

I was skeptical when Elder Michaux brought Brother Lewis into our fold. His history leaves much to be desired, and I don't mean the gambling alone. I believe he has been incarcerated for theft as well. I thought he'd bring trouble to the Church, but Brother Lewis seems to be coming along fine. He surely has a way with words and knows how to inspire, qualities that clearly run in the family.

He did a decent job as a deacon in Newport News. Now he's business manager in our Philadelphia church and serving on the board of directors of Citizens and Southern Bank. It appears he's turned his life around. Elder has that effect on people, although *he* would say it's the Lord's intervention.

Brother Lewis even settled down enough to marry Sister Willie, a true soldier of Christ, who quietly helps others behind the scenes, without seeking glory herself. Though, sadly, some have said they live more as siblings than man and wife.

MARY MICHAUX

Forgive me, Lord, my thoughts. I do not trust my husband's brother. The Scriptures say I must submit myself unto my husband, and this I do willingly and with joy. It is easy to submit to a man like Lightfoot. But he is steadfast in believing he can save his brother's lost soul.

Lewis may be able to deceive some into believing he has repented, but I see his heart. Although he has behaved himself since he came to us, he remains defiant and proud.

Sin sticks. It stays by you. You can move from north to south. You can move from east to west. You may go to distant lands, but your sin goes along. You may change your name. You may surround yourself with other circumstances, and yet, your sin remains with you. You may reform, turn over a new leaf, and lead a different life, but still your record is exactly the same. Sin may only be removed through our Lord and Savior Jesus Christ.

There are people who, the Scriptures say, "profess that they know God; but in works they deny him." These people always have something up their sleeves. They will oppose you in everything you do to promote the Kingdom of God.

Lewis may lead other souls astray. Many Church members are seduced by his cleverness and smooth talk. His verbal talents make him effective in spreading God's Word, but Satan has these qualities too.

The Lord says, "He that worketh deceit shall not dwell within my house."

LEWIS

I've been doing all right for myself and shouldn't complain, but church work isn't for me.

These people hope to go to Heaven where they can get something for nothing while everything they want is here on earth. The Negro is always looking for a job and never asks what it pays. All he wants is a job. He's been indoctrinated from the pulpit that God says be satisfied with whatever state you're in, but I can't conceive of the notion that God wants any man to be satisfied with *hungry.*

I wonder what Poppa might've told me—now that I'm looking beyond the easy buck. I keep thinking about Marcus Garvey and what he says about black people knowing themselves. It's clear that if the so-called Negro goes to school, he earns a degree for knowing the *white* man, but not for knowing *himself.* All he learns about himself is slavery. Slavery is not a history of a man; it's a misfortune of a race of people. The black man needs to know the dignity of our race. The only way he will get this knowledge is to take it for himself.

The knowledge is out there in the minds and souls of other black men. It's in the books I've been reading. The Negro needs to know about these books. He needs to read them. He needs to feel and understand the hope, the anger, and the determination that Frederick Douglass felt when he finally understood something he'd been struggling with since his youth—how the white man was able to enslave the black man. It was the day Douglass heard his master tell the mistress of the house that learning would *spoil* the best Negro in the world. That if you teach a Negro to read, he would be unfit to be a slave.

Well, Douglass got that message and set about learning to read. Ol' Frederick had more upstairs than most black men today, and that was before he could read. When he learns, he doesn't stop there. He teaches other slaves in secret. Says it's the delight of his soul to be doing something to better the condition of his race.

I try to talk with Willie about this. She smiles and nods and reads her Bible. Lightfoot meant well, but if it wasn't for me, Willie would have married that other man she'd set her cap for. Now she's a bride of the Church.

Religion can be a good thing. Churches did black folks good after Reconstruction. It was the only place people like Nat Turner and Douglass could hold meetings to unite our people. But the white man wanted to teach black folks about the by and by in the sky. He wanted to take their minds off the things here, so maybe they wouldn't notice who was kicking them in the head.

I admit, since joining my brother, I've changed some of my views. But you have to be smart about religion. You have to look closely at who's claiming it and how they're using it.

Douglass says it was necessary to keep the masters ignorant of the fact their slaves were trying to learn how to read the word of God.

Frederick Douglass, 1850

Masters would rather see them "spending the Sabbath in wrestling, boxing, and drinking whisky" than "behaving like intellectual, moral, and accountable beings."

Douglass wasn't against religion, just the misuse of it. He was something, that man—sharp as a razor.

When I first came to Lightfoot's church, I was reading the Bible mostly. Making good use of the eye I got left. Knowing Scripture is important and useful, but you can eat onions so long that you don't even believe carrots are good 'cause you've just become an onion. I'm seeing that you can't understand the Bible without considering it in the context of other ideas. People should be balanced in their thinking.

Damn. Wish I could spend an evening with Poppa talking about it all.

LIGHTFOOT

Lewis has come a long way, but I sense he is still controlled by ideas that run counter to the interests of the Church. On several occasions, I have had to mediate his conflicts with Church officials. Lewis has always had trouble with authority, but he needs to learn we must all submit to a divine power or, in the end, lose our very souls to the Evil One. We first begin to learn this ultimate submission by deferring to worthy authorities here on earth.

But I must tread lightly. I know those trips Lewis has been taking to New York have been about much more than Church business or visiting family in Port Chester. My heart tells me he's restless and looking for options—a dangerous state of mind for my brother. I don't want to lose him again.

LEWIS

I believe in God, and I love my brother. But I don't want any religion that will demand I lose my individuality.

It was one thing for me to butt heads with the deacons, but Mary is Lightfoot's wife. When she called me to read that Scripture before the congregation, I know she wanted to make an example of me, to show that I must be dutiful. She selected those particular passages intentionally.

For the grace given unto me, to every man that is among you, not to think of himself more highly than he ought to think.

Unto the pure all things are pure: but unto them that are defiled and unbelieving is nothing pure; but even their mind and conscience is defiled.

By telling me to read those words of self-condemnation, Mary wanted to humiliate me. When I refused, Lightfoot took her side. Time for me to go.

Willie isn't coming. No surprise there.

Even if I wanted to stay, Lightfoot would never allow it unless I change. Willie, Lightfoot, and Mary—all want to change me. Maybe I could use some changing but to what?

I've been making some contacts in New York City while on Church business there. Harlem seems to be the place where black men are making their voices heard. Building something of their own. And with my sister Margaret in the city and Poppa's sister, Aunt Sadie, nearby in Port Chester, I wouldn't be alone.

I'm feeling my life is there.

MARY MICHAUX

Some think we can be Christians and sinners at the same time. They believe they can be Christians falling and rising, in and out, sinning and confessing continually. But we are taught to abide in Christ, and that does not mean in and out.

LIGHTFOOT

Mary has made it clear I should wash my hands of my brother. But the Lord must be pushing me toward him as I can't turn away.

When Lewis left for New York, I was hopeful that our sister Margaret and Aunt Sadie would provide some stability for him there. I am deeply disappointed to learn he is back to his Godless ways—gambling, and possibly even dealing in drugs and women. It is exasperating because Lewis could do great things if his energies were properly channeled.

I pray for guidance on the next step to take on behalf of my brother.

SECTION 3
1937–1945

I AM NOT
A
SO-CALLED
NEGRO

LEWIS

HARLEM

I was right to leave Lightfoot's church, but I can't deny there was comfort in his world. Even here in Harlem, there's not much for an upright black man. I've tried, but the pickings are slim and there's always money to be had out on the street. Lightfoot tells me I'm making a deal with the Devil. I guess it don't matter much. I'm already in hell.

The other day a fella asked me to make some deliveries for a nice chunk of money. I don't know the man, but I've heard he's a drug-pushing pimp. I didn't have to ask, but I did anyway.

"What's the merchandise?"

"You kiddin' me, man!" was all he said.

I draw the line at cards and dice. I turned him down, but I was tempted. And it scared me. You can't work in a fish factory and don't stink.

Seems I left the pulpit for the snake pit.

LIGHTFOOT

WASHINGTON, D.C.

Although Mary is in disagreement with me, I hope to convince Lewis to join my farm project—the National Memorial to the Progress of the Colored Race in America. The land we purchased—over five hundred acres in Virginia where slaves of the first white settlers worked—has made this possible. Our project will honor the Negro leadership that has blazed the trail up from slavery. Praise the Lord.

A recruiting office in New York would draw many, and I know Lewis could make it a success if he saw its merits. I may have had unrealistic expectations of him with regard to his commitment to the Church. This project, even though church-related, is better suited to Lewis's nature. It might give him some of the independence he so craves.

PROGRAM FOR THE NATIONAL MEMORIAL TO THE PROGRESS OF THE COLORED RACE IN AMERICA

GOLDEN GATE AUDITORIUM
NEW YORK, NY

Colored man, your time is up for complaining about what the white man is not doing for you. Fourteen million colored people live in America, the richest country on earth, without an economic program for their future. Their children are being educated, coming out of school by the thousands, year after year, with no jobs to receive them but those of porter, redcap, waiter, cook, chauffeur, or a domestic of some kind.

Let us do something about it for we have brain and brawn as much as any of the other groups that live in America. Let us organize to overcome our economic condition with a program that is worthy.

Do you know that Harlem with its 325,000 colored citizens can be turned into a colored state and be owned and controlled by colored people? Do you know that the colored people who live in Harlem are the purchasers of every building in Harlem, the supporters of every business, and the payees of all the taxes that are levied on all the properties in Harlem? Colored man, you have purchased every house in Harlem a dozen times without ever being given a title to one-tenth of 1 percent of the real estate in Harlem. Colored man, you have caused the success of every prosperous business in Harlem. Colored man, you have paid every dime of the licenses for the business and all income tax on profits made in the businesses of Harlem, without sharing one-tenth of 1 percent of the profits therefrom. One hundred percent of these profits should go to you.

Therefore, I'm here to tell you that the people in any community who pay rent to a landlord and who represent the purchasing power upon which business in that community must exist are the people who should own and control that community as a race of people, especially that majority who are all of any particular race. For instance, in Chinatown, New York, as well as Chinatown, San Francisco, both areas are small, but you will find in them all the necessities that can be procured in any other section of the city, and 100 percent of the persons working in these places are Chinese.

We know of many cities in which there are Negro districts where the business is conducted almost wholly by members of other races. It is my contention that if other minority groups can carry on business among themselves in this country and turn the monies that they earn into their own investments and employment, certainly the Negroes of Harlem can follow the same policy or else their labor will become chattel to be bought and sold without any standard value.

The Negro will be allowed just enough to keep a roof over his head and not enough to feed his family unless his wife finds some form of employment to help carry on. And as old age steals upon him, the future becomes darker and darker, and unless he has children to support him, he will be subject to charity.

There have been many suggestions by our friends as well as our enemies to colonize us on some spot of uninhabited land or to send us back to Africa to work out our problems. This never has interested me in the least, and I am sure it has never interested the rest of colored Americans for we are still here.

Let me inform you that I am not a new Moses who heard the voice of God say out of the burning bush, "Go lead my colored children out of America to some foreign land, flowing with milk and honey." But we want to start tonight a campaign under the auspices of the National Memorial to the Progress of the Colored Race in America to build an economic foundation for the support of an intragovernment, which we shall build in America.

The plan is as follows. . . .

LEWIS

Lightfoot is determined. Still trying to make a respectable citizen of his brother. But his new venture does interest me. A self-sufficient black community feels like something Garvey would approve of.

Lightfoot wants me to recruit families to move to Virginia and work the land. He's already arranged an office on Seventh Avenue, right in the heart of Harlem. When my brother wants something, he won't be denied. Lightfoot may have more of Poppa in him than I realized. Maybe he's found a cause that suits us both. Feels better than this other mess I've been mired in.

1938

LEWIS

I am not a so-called Negro. I say "so-called" because a Negro is a thing, not a person. The word is an invention. A Negro is a thing to be used, abused, accused, and refused. That's his role in this stroll. And blacks who continue to accept this ain't going nowhere. 'Cause it was these so-called Negroes who helped perpetuate slavery.

Ask me a year ago why the black man can't succeed and I would have said because of white oppression. Ask me now and I'd have to add because he doesn't know himself.

This recruiting business has put me in touch with a lot of black folks, and brother, it's a crime how few really know their own history. If a man don't know where he's come from, he don't know where he's going. If you don't know what you're worth, you don't know what to charge for your labor. You gotta know who you are before you can improve your condition.

The black man is asleep. No, he's not asleep. He's awake. He's sitting on the edge of the bed scratching.

LIGHTFOOT

I had high hopes for the Memorial, but finding families to commit to the project is more challenging than I expected. I'm not ready to abandon the venture, but perhaps I should rethink my strategy.

Even for those who share the vision, that old disabler fear is an obstacle. Risk is something that requires faith, and sadly, the need for this is great.

Happy News, the publication of Lightfoot's Church of God, from 1938

LEWIS

Just as I'm putting down roots, Lightfoot decides to close this office and focus on other towns. Guess I should have seen this coming. Most folks who came to the recruitment office didn't really get the concept of the Memorial. It was impossible to persuade them to buy in. And the more I think on it, the more I see they were right. We can't be asking these New York blacks to pick up and move to some field in Virginia. They don't know farming. These are city folks. They belong right here. And I belong with them.

People are still struggling to recover from the Depression. But the soul of Harlem showed itself before the crash. Fools say, "Those were the good old days, and they're gone." Well, what blacks need to be doing now is talking about the good *new* days ahead.

I keep coming back to the same thing. Knowledge. Our people need to continue on the climb Douglass started. They need to read. I'm talking about books you don't find in just any bookstore. Books *for* black people, books *by* black people, books *about* black people here and all around the world. The so-called Negro needs to hear and learn from the voices of black men and women.

This office would be perfect for a bookstore. *My* bookstore.

A Harlem Banker

I don't know what these people expect. We cannot lend money to just anybody who comes along with a whim. We need some guarantees.

Like that Negro, Lewis Michaux. He comes in and asks to borrow five hundred dollars to open a bookstore in Harlem. He says he wants to sell books "by and about black people."

Well, I gave him a taste of reality.

"You can make out an application, but I can tell you where it's going."

"Where?" Michaux asked.

"Nowhere," I said.

He didn't get it. I told him Negroes don't read.

To his credit, Michaux acknowledged this fact. I had reached out my hand to bid him good-bye before I realized he still hadn't changed his mind. Stubborn. Going on about how he planned to *get* Negroes to read and spouting things like, "If you know, you can grow," and other such nonsense.

Michaux's dumber than he looks if he thinks one little bookstore is going to change the Negro condition. The man has no experience in the book business. I suspect he hasn't had much education. A store like that wouldn't last six months in Harlem. Michaux would lose his shirt and *our* five hundred dollars. I must admit, he had a good line—even had me laughing a couple of times, but I still sent him packing for his own good— and the bank's.

Now if he wanted to open a place to sell fried chicken or chitterlings, we could do business. Negroes eat up that kind of stuff.

LIGHTFOOT

Mary has warned me once again about putting faith in Lewis's redemption. She believes his soul is lost.

But his bookstore plan is noble. Lewis seems intent on being a force for positive change in the community. He sees the need for Negro people to be educated, to know their history. In this, there is hope. Lewis has a solid business sense and he's a good salesman. Poppa would want me to encourage this enterprise.

My Harlem recruitment office will make a fine store location. Mary insists I give Lewis no financial help, reminding me that our funds are for the Lord's work. But this could very well *be* His work. Giving Lewis a push in a positive direction can only help him avoid returning to his life of sin.

I'll continue to pay the rent for a few more months, but after that I expect him to take on the responsibility. He needs to do this on his own, but he is my brother and seemingly making an effort. It would be unchristian of me to refuse him.

LEWIS

Well, Lightfoot bought me some time to get things going here, no thanks to Mary. He was pleased when I told him I'd honor his farm project and call it the National Memorial African Bookstore. I'm also keeping the paintings of the African heads of state up on the walls. The way I see it, the foundation of this store will be the people who came before.

I've got the place. Now I need the books. Seems most publishers aren't interested in books about blacks, and the Depression has made them cautious. It won't be easy, but I'm going to do this or I'm not my father's son.

There are people who don't understand what I'm trying to do. They don't matter. I've got folks who are helping. Some let me comb through books in their basements. Said I could take what I wanted for my inventory. I found Booker T. Washington's *Up from Slavery* and four others on Harriet Tubman, Sojourner Truth, Mary McLeod Bethune, and George Washington Carver. So I've got five books, a building, and a hundred bucks.

I'm starting my business tomorrow.

Philadelphia Banker Richard Wright

I remember Lewis Michaux when he was deacon of the Church of God here. He was on our board of directors for a time. Not someone a person would be likely to forget. Clever, ambitious, a bit rebellious. Ultimately there was some kind of break with the church. A clash of personalities, I believe. But there was something about Lewis. He was his own man. Likable too. Now he's trying to sell books in Harlem and asking me for a business loan.

   I did some checking. A New York fellow I talked with told me he'd seen Lewis walking up and down 125th Street selling books from a pushcart. Apparently he is also washing windows to make ends meet. He's obviously not afraid of hard work and shows some tenacity in this book enterprise.

   As a Philadelphia bank, Harlem is out of my lending area, but sometimes rules should be broken for worthy causes.

Richard R. Wright enters the Citizens and Southern Bank, which he founded in Philadelphia in 1921.

Lightfoot *(far right)* shares a stage with President Franklin D. Roosevelt *(second from left)*.

LEWIS

Thanks to old man Wright, I finally got more books into the store. Just in time too. Lightfoot cut me off. That church of his is bringing in all kinds of money. He's got real-estate investments and has gotten friendly with the Roosevelts and other bigwigs. Lightfoot's got means and influence but won't give me a quarter. Says his money belongs to the Lord and he isn't about to give it to the Devil. Seems he's objecting to some of the books I'm selling—books on playing the numbers and some about sex. I say, if you want to read a real racy book, read the Bible. If a sexy book gets them in the door, I'll show them a sexy book. Then I'll show them Douglass or DuBois or something else of value. If you're in the book business, you've got to sell books.

It's hard though. Most of our people are just trying to pay the bills. It's tough to get them to even look in the window, much less come into the store. That's why I'm back to doing what Lightfoot and I did for Poppa's fish business—movin' my feet and takin' the goods to the streets. Still don't get many takers. I'm lucky to make a dollar a day or even six bits. Sometimes I wonder if it's worth it.

Yesterday, a man came by and asked, "Are you Elder Michaux's brother?"

I said, "Yeah."

"Well, you're crazy!" the man said. "I was in Washington last Sunday, and your brother had twenty-five thousand people in Griffith Stadium singing, 'Happy Am I,' and they were dropping half dollars and dollar bills and even checks in the collection baskets. Here you are, up in Harlem, washing windows and trying to sell a Negro a book. You've got to be kidding."

Well, I couldn't argue with the man. Sometimes it makes no sense even to me. Lightfoot is down there selling property in Heaven, which people gladly buy. And here I am.

I'm thinking the way to hide something from the black man is to put it in a book. It's a shame.

But I just keep on being crazy and sleeping in the cellar and eating soup at the Chock full o'Nuts coffee shop across the street.

I just keep on.

I'm thankful for one difference from those days selling fish. I like the smell of books.

LEWIS

JUNE We lost one of the greats. Garvey's gone. He died way over in England, but we're feeling it here. Gone, but I hope never forgotten.

I'll carry on his message—Back to Africa. Blacks in this country *should* go. Go see Africa, *learn* about it, learn *from* it. Stay if you want, but you don't have to.

Truth is, the whole continent of Africa is governed by white people. And down in the West Indies, beautiful places like Bermuda—when you see somebody with a white collar on and a pen writing something, he's white. When you see a black man, he's got a mop and a broom. Black people in this country aren't what the slavers stole. We don't fit in Africa anymore. I'm placing my bet on the opportunity right here.

My bookstore can be a boot camp for the cause.

Harlem Street Vendor

Michaux's got a storefront, but he must not be getting many customers. Just about every day he's walking up and down the street selling books. Or trying to.

Me, I just set up my table and wait for customers to come. This guy parks a cart of books on the corner and calls out, "Don't get took! Read a book! Come on by and take a look!" He'll stop people and talk to them about reading. After a while, he moves to another spot and starts yelling something else like, "If this selection isn't perfection, there's more at my store!" Guess he thinks you have to be some kind of actor to get business.

Not me. I do all right, just sitting here. 'Course I'm not trying to sell books. People always buy smokes.

Michaux can lay it on pretty thick, but I don't think he's making much. Last week, I saw him at Chock full o'Nuts counting out change to pay for a grilled cheese sandwich. Didn't have enough, so he offered to wash their windows. The cashier paid the difference.

1941

LEWIS

I don't pray anymore. When I first started out with Lightfoot in the
Church, I had but three books. A hymn book, a Bible book, and an empty
pocketbook waiting on the Lord. I found out by reading other books who
the Lord is. I read up on all the gods in all religions, and I found out who
the real Lord is. That is the *landlord*. He comes to see me every month.
So praying doesn't get it. Work gets it. And I'm working hard.

LEWIS

MARCH Mother finally got some peace. What a life she had. Eleven of us, plus the four babies who died. Seems she was either chasing after children or being chased after, and scrubbing floors in between. No wonder her nerves were shot. She went to her Maker happy though. Lightfoot, her pride and joy, gave her that.

I know I was mostly just trouble for her, but she said she loved me. Maybe someday I'll make her proud.

Death certificate for Blanche Michaux

1943

LEWIS

After years of living in Pittsburgh, Norris has decided to move his family to New York. Not the city. He and Sinah are moving to Aunt Sadie's house in Port Chester. It'll be good for Sadie. She's been a widow woman for a while now and getting on in years. I'm sure she could use some help with that big old place.

Norris has been traveling back and forth looking for work. I told him he could partner with me in the bookstore, but he wasn't having it. He laughed and said, "What? You a Boy Scout now? This is *me* you're talking to." He doesn't understand what I'm trying to do.

My little brother's got a pool cue in his back pocket, always hoping to make a bet. Looking for fast money. But I heard Sinah wouldn't leave Pittsburgh unless Norris had a nine-to-five, so he must have found some kind of job. He changed the subject when I asked, so I didn't push it.

It'll be nice to have more family around.

NORRIS

It's good to be in New York to stay. Pittsburgh's okay, but Sinah's family was always up in my business. It was like living in a fish bowl.

Aunt Sadie and Sinah are peas in a pod, so catfights won't be a problem. Sinah's smart about letting Sadie have the last word.

It's obvious that Lightfoot had a hand in financing this house. His stamp is all over it. The place is so huge, privacy won't be an issue. And as my boys get out of the service, there'll be room for them . . . and their families, when the time comes.

Making some dough is the thing now. In Pittsburgh, Sinah let me get away with working the billiard table. I've mastered that one thing and she knows it. I was bringing home some scratch. When money *was* tight, she let me slide 'cause there was still some support from her family.

But she made it plain she wasn't coming to New York unless I had a "real job." Her words, not mine. So I took this situation at the American Felt Company just across the border in Glenville, Connecticut. It's factory work, but at least I'll be on the graveyard shift. I like the night.

Lewis wanted me to throw in with him. But selling books? To colored folks? I may be a gambling man, but not when the odds of winning are zero.

Norris Michaux in the 1940s

LIGHTFOOT

I have to give Lewis credit. He's making his mark with that bookstore of his. Granted, not always in the way I'd like, but I've been hearing mostly good regarding the impact of the store on the Harlem community. And more important to me personally, the business seems to be providing Lewis with purpose.

In this way my prayers for my brother have been answered. I don't much care for some of the books he's selling, but I've known Lewis long enough to realize there are certain things that are beyond my control.

I worry less about him now that our sisters Margaret and Ruth are working in the store. Lewis showed some wisdom in hiring them. Even that pretty Batch girl, who Norris's son is set on marrying, is on the staff. There's something especially rewarding about a family business. Poppa would approve.

Now if Lewis would pay closer attention to the statements he makes, the causes he supports, and the company he keeps, he might end up doing quite well, in spite of himself.

Bookstore flier

OLIVE BATCH, Store Bookkeeper

Mail-order business at the store is really picking up. More and more families are sending books to overseas soldiers. And since we've started mailing out our catalogs, we have so many college and university orders I can hardly keep up.

I know some people in the Michaux family think poorly of Lewis, mainly because of some shady activities in his past. But I watch him as he works in the store. He enjoys people and seems happiest when he's among them, helping them, and talking about books and about life.

I like Lewis. He's not two-faced like some. He is who he is.

The bookstore on October 16, 1945, *left to right:* Lewis, Margaret Banks (Lewis's sister), Olive Batch, and an unnamed store employee

SECTION 4
1946–1956

THE HOME OF PROPER PROPAGANDA

Chicago Entrepreneur

I am interested in going into the book business and approached Carter G. Woodson for guidance. His stellar reputation in scholarly circles and connection with the *Negro History Journal* led me to his doorstep.

"I'm a historian. I'm a writer. I'm not a seller of books," Mr. Woodson said when I met with him. "The man you need to interview about Negro book sales is Michaux in New York."

Woodson was right. Lewis Michaux knows about books . . . and selling. And he shared his knowledge with enthusiasm. A trifle self-impressed but a fascinating man, and his National Memorial African Bookstore is a literary treasure.

Gus Travers,
New York City Newspaper Reporter
(OFF THE RECORD)

There's been some buzz about a place up in Harlem, and my editor sent me over to check on it. Turns out the National Memorial African Bookstore, with the exception of such things as dictionaries and Bibles, sells only books by and about black people. The shop is certainly a point of interest, but the real draw is the owner.

The first impression you get of Lewis Michaux is from the signs he's put outside. One banner above the entrance says, "World History Book Outlet on 2,000,000,000 Africans and Non-White Peoples" and includes pictures of African leaders and people like the black nationalist Marcus Garvey, the man who was trying to get American Negroes to go back to Africa. Garvey was not a person who many influential Negroes supported, so this Michaux character is clearly not part of the mainstream. Nor is he a political fence-sitter.

The sign that seems to attract the most attention reads "The House of Common Sense and the Home of Proper Propaganda." When this reporter asked Michaux what it meant, he said, "Even truth carries a propaganda." Another store sign reads "This House Is Packed with All the Facts About All the Blacks All Over the World." Even if you call it bad poetry, you only have to stand outside for five minutes to see its effect. People point and laugh and start talking and many go inside.

Michaux is small, but you wouldn't miss him in a room of a thousand people. His quick wit and sharp tongue might be intimidating if he weren't such an everyman. Michaux's got a rare kind of charm. He's a born salesman with a passion for books, but more than that, he's a kind of storefront philosopher. People call him the Professor. When I asked why, he said, "I am a professor in my own field. I have nothing against college knowledge, but don't overlook the experience of a man who has lived with a thing. You see," he said, "I don't have to pull no punches. I don't stammer. I don't talk from no manuscript like a trained Negro has to talk so he'll be sure not to offend the folks whose shoes he's shining."

It seems Michaux has an opinion on everything and isn't shy about sharing it.

This reporter is expecting to hear more about him in the future.

LEWIS

Many so-called Negroes been asking me about Garvey. They don't really want to know about the man. They're asking more as a challenge. They want me to explain him, defend him. They don't get the importance of Garvey or his movement.

Garvey was a brilliant individual. The things Garvey said, you couldn't rub 'em off. They stuck. When a man is doing a thing, he has to do it the way he sees it. The trouble Garvey had was from within. At that time, DuBois and all those outstanding professional Negroes were against him because he advocated Back to Africa. Garvey was bigger than anything those educators could come up with, and they had to dispose of him. They couldn't have him coming in getting the attention of millions of people when they couldn't.

At the time, nobody was talking any philosophy about our heritage, our background. Naturally, Garvey clicked. But the structure had to get rid of him. People got jealous, and they sicced the dogs on him. All those people were against Garvey because he had a tangible program.

And he wasn't for sale.

LEWIS

Sparks from the Anvil arrived today. A fitting title. One of his church members decided to put together the little sayings Lightfoot's been dropping into his sermons over the years. Many of the entries are unremarkable, but some are real gems:

> *If there's no Devil, who gets the credit for raising all the hell?*

> *Be willing to help anybody who is down, but don't go down helping him.*

> *You have got to have sense to make dollars.*

> *The Devil is a great ventriloquist; don't be his dummy.*

> *You can't do wrong and get by long.*

Guess I'm not the only poet in the family, or bookseller.

I don't always agree with Lightfoot, but he's certainly skilled with words and understands the force behind them—a quality shared by many great men.

LEWIS

I should get Langston in for a book signing. His new poetry collection, *Montage of a Dream Deferred*, is strong medicine. His way of speaking simply and honestly about black life cuts straight to the bone. I don't think he's rolling in dough, but he seems to be eating higher on the hog. People are reading him. And he's earned it . . . was only eighteen when he wrote "The Negro Speaks of Rivers." He's gotta be fifty now.

When we first met, back in the day, Hughes made almost no money writing. He was trying to establish himself as a poet and it was hard going. He said he appreciated me starting up something that would make a market for black writing.

He still stops by now and then. Our relationship is the books, period. And that's enough.

Calvin

Walking down the street in Harlem with Pop, I see a bunch of people gathered on the sidewalk.

A man's standing on a stepladder pointing and shouting, "You can be black as a crow, you can be white like snow, but if you don't know, and you ain't got no dough, then you can't go, and that's fo' sho'!"

Pop laughs and shouts back, "That's fo' sho', brother!"

"Tell me mo'!" someone else calls out.

The man on the ladder is saying black people need to know about their history and that we should read books about *us.*

"Let's go," Pop says. "We need to pick up your grandmother."

I stand still. I want to listen to this man.

"Come on, Calvin," Pop says. "He's just trying to sell something. He owns that bookstore."

The bookman says, "If you don't have money, come into the store anyway. There's a back room. Read for nothing. School's not the only place to educate."

He looks down at me from the ladder. "If you want to get books, you can come and buy them on time."

I nod. Pop takes my hand and pulls me through the crowd.

At supper, I tell Gran about the man on the ladder.

"Might be worth stopping in there," Gran says.

I glance at Pop.

"Now, Calvin." He wipes his mouth with his napkin. "I know you like reading and all, but money doesn't just fall out of the sky."

"You could buy on layaway," Gran says.

"Yes, but . . ." Pop says.

"The man even said we could just go in the store and read if we want," I say.

"Calvin's still just a boy," Gran says, "but he keeps talking about going to college and . . ."

Pop holds his hand up in the stop position. He takes a bite of mashed potatoes. This conversation is over.

BETTIE LOGAN

I'd heard about the National Memorial African Bookstore but never had the opportunity to visit until Celia and I were staying at the Hotel Theresa. It was right across the way, so we decided to stop by.

I was impressed. The minute I walked in, I could feel the importance of the place to our people. The store is remarkable—full of the kind of literature that is rarely available elsewhere. But the owner, Mr. Lewis Michaux—*oh, my.* What a charming man. Straightforward. No-nonsense. After thirty-two years on this earth, I've had enough of men who play the usual games. Lewis Michaux treated me with respect. And he made me laugh.

Celia says he's probably old enough to be my father. He doesn't look it. And so what if he is?

LEWIS

I about choked on my coffee when she walked in. Beautiful. I hustled over before Ruth could wait on her. *Don't run. Stay cool.* I didn't want to act a fool even though I knew it was love at first sight.

When she said she was looking for a copy of Douglass's *Narrative,* I knew we were connected. This was no accident. Miss Bettie Logan came to my store for a reason.

Calvin

Pop and me go back to that bookstore. I'm not sure what changed his mind. Maybe Gran. I don't care why.

I say, "Thanks, Pop."

He smiles and says, "What was it that man said last time, 'If you don't know . . .'"

"You can't go."

The bookman is Mr. Michaux.

His store doesn't look very big from the outside, but inside, it goes on forever. It's skinny but goes way back. It's jammed with books, posters, pictures, and there're people all over, so it's hard to get through the aisles.

Picking a book, it could take all day. There are so many, everywhere—along the walls almost up to the ceiling, stacked on tables, and even on the floor. I have to watch so I don't trip as we make our way toward the back.

High up on the walls I see faces, paintings of black people. They look like they're watching over us. Pop reminds me who a few of them are, but some we don't know. Mr. Michaux says they're our ancestors.

Pop says, "My boy's been worrying me about coming here. We heard you talking outside the store a couple of weeks ago." He nods his head toward me. "Look at him. What kind of book do you think this boy should have?"

Mr. Michaux looks real close at my face. He asks to see my hands, tells me to hold them out in front of me.

"Steady," he says. Then he looks at Pop. "This boy should be a doctor."

A doctor! I wonder if I really could?

"Do you have any books on medicine?" Pop asks.

Mr. Michaux goes searching on the shelves and finds a book called *The Negro in Medicine.*

Pop buys it for me. He doesn't ask if I could read it in the store. He doesn't even ask to buy it on time.

The Negro in Medicine

By
John A. Kenney, M. D.
Medical Director, Tuskegee Institute Hospital
and Nurse Training School
General Secretary, National Medical
Association
Managing Editor, Journal of the National
Medical Association

The Negro in Medicine by John A. Kenney, M.D., 1912

BETTIE

Lewis finally asked me to dinner. Celia was right. He *is* old enough to be my father—fifty-seven. But he's youthful in both mind and body. And the extra years have given him a wisdom that younger men haven't yet attained.

After hearing someone in the store call him Professor, I asked what university he'd attended. He said comfortably that he hasn't had much formal education. It was refreshing to get an honest and unapologetic answer. Lewis may not have a degree, but he's far from unintelligent. In many ways, he has more sense than most of the educated men I know. At first I wondered how much more remarkable Lewis would be if he *had* gone to a university. But a university would have produced a different man. Lewis Michaux went to school on books and experience, without the guidance or direction of academic snobs. He chose his own path. Conceived his own interpretations. Shaped his own conclusions. This is why I think he's at home in his own skin. He hasn't settled for or conformed to anyone else's views or rules.

We're seeing each other again tomorrow. This is happening so fast. I hope I'm seeing clearly.

Harlem Teenager

Last week, I'm crossing over 125th street from the Theresa, and I see this little man hollerin', "No one can live on bread alone. We've got too many big fat fools walking around with everything in their stomachs and nothing in their heads."

I start laughin' and the man says, "Do you read, brother?"

He's lookin' right at me. I'm thinkin', *Who is this clown?* I notice somethin's off with one of his eyes. It's lookin' at me and it isn't. I think about walkin' away.

But I say, "Yeah, man, I read." I give him a look I figure will shut him up. It doesn't.

He just nods and says, "That's good." Then he asks me what's the last book I read.

Course I can't name one. The last thing I read was the want ads. There's a kid in my building reads all the time. The brothers call him Einstein. He was in my English class with that sorry-ass teacher who came to my house to talk to Ma about why I quit high school.

When I don't answer, the man says, "Come on into my store."

Don't ask me why, but I do.

Inside, the little man hands me his card. Someday I'm gonna have me a card. His name's Lewis Michaux. He starts taking books off the shelf and I'm thinkin' *So what?* Then I notice all the books are about black people.

Every one.

On every table.

Every shelf.

I'm thinkin', here's somethin' different from that Romeo and Juliet junk we had at school.

But why should I care? I just want me a job. I look at the books. Then I look at the eye I figure is fake. Why don't he cover it up with a patch or dark glasses or somethin'?

"So?" I say.

"So," says Mr. Michaux, "There's knowledge here, son. Is there something more important you have to do today than to start walking down the road to wisdom?"

"Yeah. I need to walk down the road to a job!"

"Ain't no job more important than filling your head."

He hands me a book—*The Dream Keeper and Other Poems.*

"If you need a job, you probably can't buy books," he says, "but you can read." He takes me to a back room and says, "My library."

I can't believe it. I say, "You expect me to sit here and read these poems? Right now?"

"I don't expect nothing in this world. I'm just offering you some hospitality."

I sit and open the book. What else do I have to do?

> **Bring me all your dreams,**
> **You dreamers,**

Yeah, I had dreams.

> **Bring me all your**
> **Heart melodies**
> **That I may wrap them**
> **In a blue cloud-cloth**
> **Away from the too-rough fingers**
> **Of the world.**

The too-rough fingers of the world. I sit there for a few minutes, just thinking.

I read another one.

Title page of *The Dream Keeper* by Langston Hughes, 1954

THE DREAM KEEPER
AND OTHER POEMS
LANGSTON HUGHES

Illustrations by Helen Sewell

NEW YORK: ALFRED A. KNOPF
19 54

Well, son, I'll tell you:
Life for me ain't been no crystal stair.
It's had tacks in it,
And splinters,
And boards torn up,
And places with no carpet on the floor—
Bare.
But all the time
I'se been a-climbin' on,
And reachin' landin's,
And turnin' corners,
And sometimes goin' in the dark
Where there ain't been no light.
So, boy, don't you turn back.
Don't you set down on the steps
'Cause you finds it kinder hard.
Don't you fall now—
For I'se still goin', honey,
For I'se still climbin',
And life for me ain't been no crystal stair.

Sounds like Mama—like the day we're taking the steps in our building and I say, "Ma, why don't we take the elevator? I'm tired." She says, "That elevator's for weak folks. These steps keep us strong." But I think the poem is talking about more than that.

I read all afternoon and I finish the book.

"Well?" Mr. Michaux says.

"Well, what? You want a book report or somethin'?"

"How about a brain report?" he says.

The man is something.

"Not bad." I say. "This Langston Hughes seems to know some things."

Mr. Michaux asks my name.

"Snooze," I say.

He smiles and shakes his head. "Well, Snooze." He goes to the shelf and pulls off another book. "Think you can stay awake long enough to read this one?"

What! What is with this guy? He's standing there holding out the book, looking at me. That eye again.

I walk out.

LEWIS

SEPTEMBER 6 I knew when Bettie came into the store three years ago, we were meant to be together. I was tickled when she married me, but I never imagined we'd be having a son. I'd given up on the idea of children.

Now there's Lewis Henri Michaux Jr. Too bad Mother and Poppa aren't around to spoil him. I guess I'll have to do that job for all of us.

Snooze

After I read *The Dream Keeper* at Mr. Michaux's, I go to the library to read it again. The librarian says I can borrow the book with a library card. I don't have one. Don't know if I want one. I read it there.

Man, how does Hughes know this stuff? It's like he's inside my head. Like he's reading my mind.

I, too, sing America. I read it over and over. It carves itself deep in my mind 'til it sticks. I can't shake it. Don't want to.

> *I am the darker brother.*
> *They send me to eat in the kitchen*
> *When company comes,*
> *But I laugh,*
> *And eat well,*
> *And grow strong.*
>
> *Tomorrow,*
> *I'll sit at the table*
> *When company comes.*
> *Nobody'll dare*
> *Say to me,*
> *"Eat in the kitchen,"*
> *Then.*
>
> *Besides,*
> *They'll see how beautiful I am*
> *And be ashamed—*
>
> *I, too, am America.*

I don't mean to go back to Mr. Michaux's. I just happen to be on Seventh Avenue. I walk by the store. I look in but keep walking. I don't want Michaux on my case, playin' teacher with me. But somehow, I find myself turning around and walking in.

"How goes it, Snooze?"

He remembers me. I think about leaving, but he doesn't come over. He's helping another customer.

"I'm cool," I say.

I start looking at books on the shelf. I find the poetry section. Poetry. *Man, what's wrong with me? I should be lookin' for a job.*

"Try Paul Laurence Dunbar," Mr. Michaux says from behind me. Then he walks away. He's not gonna play teacher.

I find one on the shelf—*The Complete Poems*—and start lookin' through it.

> *A crust of bread and a corner to sleep in,*
> *A minute to smile and an hour to weep in,*
> *A pint of joy to a peck of trouble,*
> *And never a laugh but the moans come double;*
> *And that is life!*

> *A crust and a corner that love makes precious,*
> *With a smile to warm and the tears to refresh us;*
> *And joy seems sweeter when cares come after,*
> *And a moan is the finest of foils for laughter;*
> *And that is life!*

I stand reading in the narrow aisle, with books all around. Mr. Michaux catches my eye and nods toward the back room. Another invitation to his "library." How does he make any money if people can just come in and read? I don't get it, but I spend another afternoon with poetry.

Seems like every week I'm stopping in. After a while, I go straight to the back. Mr. Michaux has started piling books—his picks for me—on a table by the chair I use.

The other day, I got my library card. I'm still reading at Mr. Michaux's, but I'm taking books home from the library too. I ask the librarian about jobs. She gives me some of the lowdown. Seems like the only jobs I might get are cleanin' up after people or workin' in the hot sun. Is that all there is for me? I don't want to eat in the kitchen when company comes. I want them to see how beautiful I am because I, too, am America. I'll eat well and grow strong.

Maybe goin' back to school wouldn't be so bad.

New York Resident

My husband and I were driving on Seventh Avenue through Harlem yesterday when we passed that Negro bookstore. Well, displayed right out front was a picture of our Lord Jesus Christ as a Negro. I was appalled! I had Frank stop the car so I could get out. In the window display was a ridiculous poster saying 'CHRIST WAS BLACK AS A MATTER OF FACT,' even quoting Scripture to support this horrendous notion. I wanted to scream, but I held my tongue, not wishing to make a scene. Who knows how those people might react?

Still, I had to do something. After returning home, I composed a letter to the Negro proprietor—a Mr. Lewis Michaux—and gave him a piece of my mind.

"Get all that filthy garbage out of your store and put the Lord Jesus Christ and His saving power in it," I wrote, "for if you don't, you will surely burn in Hell. For your information, there was nothing black in Him. God and the family of God are white."

It seems it is the most I can do as there are no laws against believing in a delusion. I can only pray that this man will find the one true God and beg His forgiveness.

Yes! "CHRIST WAS BLACK"
AS A MATTER OF FACT AND TO BE EXACT.
OUR LORD AND SAVIOR CHRIST WAS BLACK
And this is no onesided phoney crack. I have the proof because I know the Truth.

Moses said He was a "Lion's Whelp". Genesis 49. 9 to 10. Apostle Paul said: "He sprang out of Judah". Heb. 7—14.

Now the Tribe of Judah "Was a Tribe of Black People". A direct descendant of "Ham" and Christ came from that Tribe. John in the Isle call Patmos; Saw Him and called Him the Lion of the Tribe of Judah "And His hair was like wool". Rev. 1—14 and Rev. 5. 5.

For the complete story and His Picture, write to:
Prof. HENRI MICHEAUX
2107 7th Avenue   New York 27, N. Y.

Card printed and distributed by Lewis before 1968

Snooze

Today the Professor, that's what people call him, says to me, "Hey, Snooze. Do you have another name?"

He takes me off guard and I'm wondering where he's going.

"Why?" I ask.

"Well," he says, "don't seem like Snooze is the kind of name a mother would pick for her baby."

I feel my face get hot. "Samuel . . . Samuel Walker. And I don't like Sammy."

He nods. Now he's calling me Samuel. When he says it, it sounds like he's respecting me.

IF THE TRUTH STIRS IT UP, LET IT COME.

LEWIS

I thought after we lost Marcus Garvey, there were no black leaders left who weren't for sale, none who weren't tainted by politics, none who could still communicate with the regular folks. But Malcolm. He's got something.

When we first met, back in the forties, he didn't have it. He'd drop into Harlem now and then, struttin' around with his hair all conked. He was just a kid—Detroit Red—not yet Malcolm X. He was hustling like everybody else. It's what sent him up the river.

Prison saved him.

No.

Education saved him. Prison helped him get there, though. Says he read books from the prison library, including the dictionary. And he found direction in the Nation of Islam.

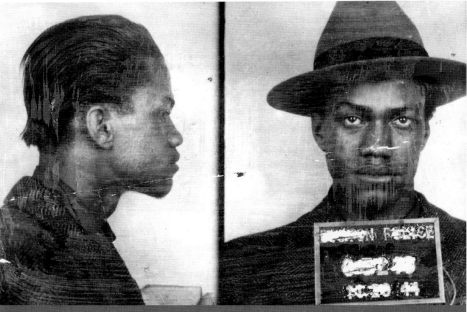

Police photos of Malcolm Little (later Malcolm X) taken after his arrest for larceny in Boston, 1944

Malcolm is a changed man. When he spoke to the crowd yesterday, it wasn't like before. I knew, finally, we have someone to pick up where Garvey left off. Malcolm's not Garvey. And that's good. Garvey had a program and a commitment, but his message didn't reach the people. He was a stepping-stone. He *conceived* of liberation, now Malcolm's come along to explain it to the people. Take DuBois. I have nothing to say against him; he is a great man. But DuBois won't speak to a regular man on the street. He'll speak to a group if you go to see him, but when you meet him on the street, you speak to *him.* He's so swelled up with college degrees, so high-toned, the ordinary man can't appreciate him.

A trained Negro is a tamed Negro—he's trained to say soft, intellectual things. He's too tame to tell about the shame.

Malcolm didn't come from Yale. He came out of jail, and I believe there isn't a Ph.D. he can't debate and prevail. He was fortunate not to have enough education to be tamed. He makes it plain. He connects with people. He's got the gift of delivery. I believe Malcolm is a great orator in the spirit of Frederick Douglass.

LIGHTFOOT
WASHINGTON, D.C.

Lewis's connection with Malcolm X and the Nation of Islam is of major concern to me. Why must he insist upon aligning himself with radicals and extremists? Director Hoover will take notice. Heaven help us if he gets entangled with the FBI.

NEW YORK REGISTER

SEPTEMBER 21, 1958

MARTIN LUTHER KING JR. STABBED AT BLUMSTEIN'S AUTOGRAPHING EVENT

BY GUS TRAVERS

The Reverend Dr. Martin Luther King Jr. was stabbed by a woman armed with a letter opener during an autographing event at Blumstein's Department Store in Harlem yesterday afternoon.

King was rushed by ambulance to the Harlem Hospital where he is recovering from a 'near-fatal' wound allegedly inflicted by Izola Curry, a well-dressed, middle-aged Negro woman. At about 3:30, according to witnesses, Curry pushed her way through the crowd of book buyers waiting in line for Dr. King to sign their copies of his newly released *Stride Toward Freedom: The Montgomery Story.* She approached the desk where Dr. King was autographing and asked, "Is this Martin Luther King?"

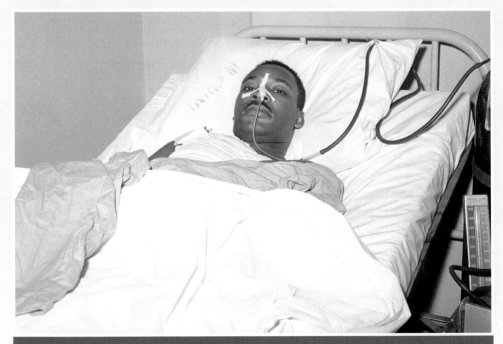

Dr. Martin Luther King Jr. recovers in a Harlem hospital after surgery to remove an assassin's letter opener from his chest.

"Yes, it is," King said.

According to police reports, Curry pulled the seven-inch, razor-sharp, Japanese letter opener from inside her raincoat and plunged it into King's chest. Onlookers overpowered the woman, who was reportedly ranting in a crazed manner, and held her until security officers arrived.

A hospital spokesman called the incident an "extremely close call" because the weapon's tip rested against the outer wall of King's aorta. He said any sudden movement prior to its removal by the surgical team could have punctured the vessel, caused internal bleeding, and threatened immediate death. If those who were with King when the attack occurred had attempted to remove the letter opener themselves, the spokesman said, the life of the young minister and civil rights leader may have come to an end.

Curry, who was arrested by police after the incident, wasn't the only person disrupting the Blumstein's event. The owner of the National Memorial African Bookstore, Lewis Michaux, and several of his supporters staged a nonviolent protest that King had held his autographing event at a business alleged not to hire Negro employees. Michaux stated he had hoped King would have scheduled a signing at his store, which does hire Negroes and offers an inventory of ethnic books.

LEWIS

What occurred at Blumstein's was a shame, but something was bound to happen with the situation on 125th. White businesses in our community refusing to hire the blacks who keep them in business? It's like Garvey said, our people need to *own* businesses and hire black employees, and blacks need to support those businesses by patronizing them. My bookstore is one of the few stores in Harlem that hires *only* blacks.

So yesterday they had Dr. Martin Luther King Jr. up there autographing his book, making money for Blumstein's, which won't hire even *one* of our people.

Well, we picketed the place with signs that said, "Buy Black" and "Dr. King, would you autograph your books in a white Alabama bookstore?" Not that we have anything against the white man, but wouldn't King want those profits to be made by us?

I've owned the leading bookstore in Harlem for *twenty* years, and King and his publishers didn't even come to see me. Now I don't think King did this knowingly. It was his sponsors. But we picketed, and during the demonstration, a deranged woman stabbed King with a letter opener. We had no part in that.

King has a wonderful program, and there's beauty in his words. But he's so educated, a common man has to carry a dictionary in his pocket to find out what the hell he's talking about.

FBI FILES
1958

The subject, LEWIS HENRI MICHAUX, is the owner of the National Memorial African Bookstore, 2107 Seventh Avenue, New York City, which store commenced business in 1939. He was formerly associated with the fish business in Newport News, Virginia.

The subject is a male Negro of light complexion; short; wears thick-framed glasses; has a glass eye in his left eye; and was born on August 4, 1895.

Unnamed source set forth information that MICHAUX prints all the material for various black nationalist groups in Harlem. Another source set forth information that MICHAUX'S bookstore sells antiwhite literature. That same source furnished information that MICHAUX is responsible for about 75 percent of the antiwhite material which is distributed in Harlem.

Specific sources and informants should be targeted against the bookstore to determine activities there and whether it is, as alleged by MICHAUX, a rallying point for black nationalists.

LEWIS

Sugar Ray Robinson comes in sometimes, and I noticed he hadn't been buying any books. So yesterday, I just had to say something.

I said, "Ray, you're a good man, middleweight champion, everybody's clapping for you, but can I crack a joke with you?"

"Yeah, bring it on," he said.

Well, Ray always keeps his hair all conked down—you know, dyed, fried, and laid to the side. I said, "Ray what you put *on* your head will rub off in your bed. It's what you put *in* your head that will last you 'til you're dead."

He laughed and said, "I get you, man."

Knowledge is the thing that is needed among the young people today. You can't protect yourself if you don't know something.

The store in the early 1960s

BLACK LIFE MAGAZINE
MAY 1959

BEST KEPT SECRETS

BY FLORENCE LEE, AROUND-THE-TOWN COLUMNIST

PLANNING A VISIT TO HARLEM?

Certainly you'll take in a show at the Apollo Theater—Duke Ellington, Count Basie, Ella Fitzgerald, Miles Davis, or Little Richard perhaps.

The Hotel Theresa, considered Harlem's best, is another obvious destination, its thirteen stories covering an entire city block along 125th Street. Maybe you're hoping to get a peek at Lena Horne, Eartha Kitt, Satchel Paige, Sammy Davis Jr. or Cassius Clay. Not impossible. Since it opened its doors to Negroes in 1940, the hotel has become the black elite's Waldorf.

Great spots to take in, without a doubt. But here's the inside scoop. Although most would call 125th the area's hub, many locals would disagree. For them, Seventh Avenue is Harlem's true main street with its shops, churches, beauty salons, theaters, nightclubs, apartment buildings, and private brownstones. The corner of 125th and Seventh, referred to as Harlem Square, is the hub of the community.

And the best kept secret in Harlem is at this hub, across the way from the Theresa—Lewis Michaux's National Memorial African Bookstore. This literary haven on Seventh Avenue carries an abundance of mainstream and underground books and pamphlets all about Negro history and culture. American Negro and African fiction, poetry, politics, philosophy, and art—you'll find it there.

Michaux's bookstore, as some call it, has become a regular stop for out-of-towners seeking treasures.

The store is no secret to locals. Many Harlemites are attracted to the establishment for more than reading materials. They come for the talk. Ideas and opinions are never in short supply thanks to Lewis Michaux, a small man with big ideas. Michaux's often-controversial philosophies and sense of humor keep discussions lively and bring regulars back day after day to share opinions or try to have the last word. Langston Hughes, Claude McKay, Zora Neale Hurston, James Baldwin, W.E.B. DuBois, Adam Clayton Powell Jr., Louis Armstrong, and John Henrik Clarke are among those who have frequented the store for good books and hot conversation.

And the discussions don't occur only within the walls of the National Memorial African Bookstore. The sidewalk in front of the store has become a rallying point for speeches on civil rights, education and politics. Michaux frequently takes the platform himself, black nationalism and self-sufficiency among the topics of his fiery discourse. Some speakers draw thousands of listeners and prompt police to line the streets. The crowds shout and clap to the rhythm of the rhetoric and sometimes grow so quiet one wonders at the power of the words being spoken.

The store owner says, "My primary mission is to put books into the hands of black people." He seems to be accomplishing this and more.

So, if you want to experience *all* of Harlem, the *best* of Harlem, visit Michaux's and join the discussion. Just remember to bring along your keenest arguments and plan to come away thinking.

BETTIE

I loved being able to stay home with Lewis Jr. and watch him grow up. But I've missed working, getting out more. Doing the bookkeeping at home helped, but now that he's in school, I can again spend my days at the bookstore.

Lewis seems pleased to have me here. And I'm greatly relieved. Sometimes he doesn't close the store until after ten. If customers are still looking at books, he waits until they're ready to leave. He'd never put people out because it's past closing time. While I admire his dedication to the business, those twelve-hour days meant loneliness for me. Now that I'm working at the store, I have more time with the man who is still my heart's desire.

FBI FILES
1959

On February 15, 16, 17, and 18, 1959, LEWIS HENRI MICHAUX, owner of the National Memorial African Bookstore, 2107 Seventh Avenue, New York City, attended the Committee for Negro History and Culture Bazaar, a committee which sponsors events concerning lectures and displays of Negro history.

MICHAUX operated a booth from which he distributed literature at this bazaar. He also had prints for sale showing a black Christ. MICHAUX handed out literature from the National Memorial African Bookstore, 2107 Seventh Avenue, New York City. He also distributed a booklet entitled "Integration or Liberation" at the above bazaar.

Gus Travers,
New York City Newspaper Reporter
(OFF THE RECORD)

Lewis Michaux's inclination to speak his mind are ruffling some feathers. Although he is a respected businessman and his National Memorial African Bookstore has become a Harlem institution, there are those who are calling the store a hate station.

Last week local police visited the store to investigate a sign outside promoting a book entitled *The Goddam White Man.* This reporter was on the scene when police arrived.

"Look, Michaux," one of the officers said, "enough of a thing's enough. We're getting complaints from white people who drive by here. They're saying you are agitating the situation. You have an institute of learning here," the officer said, "and this is a bad thing for young folks to be seeing—you cursing the white man. Even your own people don't like it."

"Well," Michaux replied, "what's the matter with the sign? It's a published book. I'm going to sell the book as long as the publisher is publishing it. Go see the publisher and stop him. Then I won't sell the book."

The officers left, but soon after, Michaux received a summons to appear in court and show cause for not removing the sign.

This reporter was at the courthouse the day of the hearing.

When the presiding judge asked Michaux who was representing him, he said, "I represent myself."

"That sign is disturbing the peace," the judge said. "What have you got to say for yourself?"

"I haven't got anything to say for myself particularly," Michaux replied, "but I want to say something about the police."

"What about them?"

"They can't read," the bookseller said. Then he placed a book on the bench. "I got one book that I'm going to display here before you, Your Honor, and that's Webster's Dictionary."

"What does that have to do with the case?" the judge asked.

"A lot," Michaux said. "I got a copy of the sign that's in front of my store. It says G-o-d-d-a-m White Man. That means 'he's dammed up somewhere.' It doesn't have an *n* in it."

The judge looked at the sign and said, "Well, I'll be damned!"

Despite the judge's obvious amusement, he ruled that the sign promoted racial hatred, no matter how it was spelled, and ordered Michaux to remove it.

Michaux complied, but I suspect this won't be the last time there's controversy involving the spirited bookstore owner and his literary establishment. You can bet this reporter will be there.

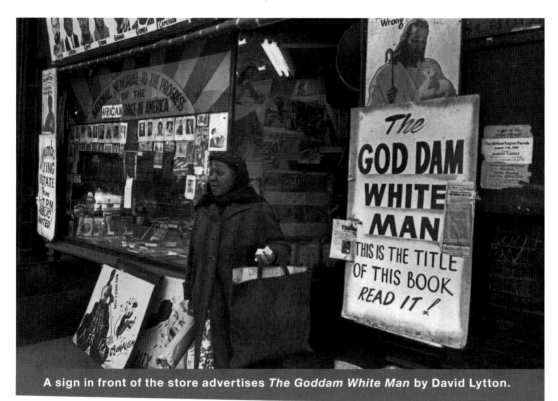

A sign in front of the store advertises *The Goddam White Man* by David Lytton.

LEWIS

I guess that judge got more than he bargained for. Hell, when I put the sign out there, I knew there'd be trouble. If I wake up in the morning and ain't nothing happening, I make something happen. I love trouble. If I wake up and don't have no trouble, trouble's got to happen.

Yeah, I took the sign down. Sometimes you got to play the politics. I'm just trying to sell books here.

James E. Turner

Lewis Michaux loves a great argument, so there is always active discussion going on at the store. You never know who you are going to meet there—authors, educators, heads of state. It is a major center of Black nationalist thought and political activity.

During one recent conversation, Mr. Michaux shared an expression he'd heard: *Slaves and pets are named by their masters. Free men name themselves.*

I believe this is what he means when he refers to the "so-called Negro." Michaux is making a clear distinction between Blacks who accept their past subservience and the new Blacks who reject that role.

Mr. Michaux wants Blacks to know their African Heritage, their historical lineage. The Negro has no history, but Africans do.

LEWIS

The so-called Negro never grows. You can't organize him.

Black people today want to be something, and they realize the value of unity.

LIGHTFOOT

I know I must accept the fact that a new breed of young black leaders has emerged and is gathering followers as I did in my early days. I give them credit, but I don't have to support them. I worked hard to build my ministry and my supporters. Now these seem to be diminishing. Well, I won't accept that. I must do everything I can to protect the Church of God and its members from Satan who walks freely among us.

It doesn't help that Eisenhower is gone. Though Ike was never as welcoming to me as Roosevelt or Truman, he had some awareness of the voters I influenced and so treated me with respect. But Kennedy appears interested only in the new breed. Men like King. It seems to me that King and those calling themselves civil rights activists and black nationalists only serve to widen the gap between blacks and whites in America.

Granted, I suspect we are all working toward the same goals—racial pride and advancement for our people. But their methods offend me, and if *I* am offended, other reasonable and influential men—men who can *do* something for us—will be as well.

Lewis is among them, touting the likes of Malcolm X, a breeder of hate. Though intelligent, Lewis is sometimes intemperate. He won't listen to me. But if he could see for himself the true nature of the Muslim organization, he might terminate this connection. Perhaps if I could expose or discredit the group in some public way, my brother would take notice.

WASHINGTON CHRONICLE
SEPTEMBER 11, 1961

RELIGIOUS DEBATE DRAWS 5,000

BY DON FOX

Washington, D.C.—As many as 5,000 people assembled at Griffith Stadium yesterday to hear what some attendees called an "historic debate" of Christianity versus Islam.

Elder Lightfoot Solomon Michaux of the Radio Church of God spoke on behalf of Christianity. Elijah Muhammad, leader of the Black Muslims, defended the Nation of Islam (NOI).

Muhammad advocated devotion to Allah and a separate state for Negroes where they could do something for themselves, not "beg (whites) for justice." He said, "I did not come to debate, but to teach."

He called blacks who are willing to integrate with whites "fools" saying, "No other people on earth would want to marry the daughters of their slave masters." Muhammad said he and those in the NOI "don't want no Uncle Toms (servile Negro leaders) appointed by a white government to rule over us." The NOI leader told Michaux, "If you really practice Christianity, you and I are brothers because Jesus was a prophet of Allah, God of all." He asserted that the worst sins committed by Christians have been to enslave others.

Michaux said that sinners who claimed to be Christians were not recognized by Christ. He told the audience he was "glad to live in a country where President Franklin Delano Roosevelt's Four Freedoms—freedom of speech, of worship, from want, and from fear—prevail, and where a man like the honorable Elijah Muhammad can say what he just said. If Mr. Muhammad wants to recognize God as Allah, it's all right with me. Let the Muslims have their God, the Hebrews have their God, and the Christians have their God." Michaux called the teachings of Islam "divisive" and declared that a good Christian would be recognized by any religion.

The schedule was delayed nearly two hours in part due to the length of time it took Muhammad's bodyguards, known as the Fruit of Islam, to search people for weapons. They politely frisked everyone, including Michaux and any clergy and their wives who had been invited to sit on the platform. Those leaving the stadium were searched again before being permitted to reenter. Malcolm X, Muhammad's spokesman, called the searches "routine procedure."

The Fruit of Islam policed the stadium—patrolling the roof, the empty bleachers, the outfields, and along the baselines—while metropolitan police, who had prepared for a larger turnout, remained outside.

Muhammad's late arrival added to the delay. Muslim followers—including the Fruit of Islam honor guard dressed in dark suits, white shirts and white bow ties—were a heavy majority. As Muhammad entered the stadium, his supporters clapped rhythmically but were countered by Michaux's integrated flock singing "Stand Up, Stand Up for Jesus."

Both religious leaders were cheered and applauded by the entire crowd as they were introduced.

While waiting for the debate to begin, the audience was entertained by lively hymns played and sung by Michaux's band and his white-robed choir. The band's jazz arrangement of the hymn, "Tramp, Tramp, Tramp of the Army," delighted the crowd for a good ten minutes.

Following the event, Michaux and Muhammad paused on stage for photographs with their wives. Mary Michaux wore a modest, print dress along with white gloves and a corsage. Clara Muhammad donned a white Muslim-style gown, white head veil, and gloves. The couples posed together briefly—the men seemed satisfied, their wives, uneasy.

Young Activist

Elder Michaux must be some kind of chump. My Pops says he was hip twenty years ago. But man, this is 1961! He needs to face the music. His time is up. Why do you think they call him ELDer?

I'm not saying Elijah Muhammad is my man. He can make sense, but there's something about him that gives me the creeps. Seems to think a little too much of himself. And the way his cronies fall all over him, lick his feet, like he's some kind of god.

But Malcolm. Malcolm, he's solid.

King's got some good things to say. But he's too hung up on integration. I wonder if he'll sell out before it's all over.

Malcolm. He speaks from the heart, man. He speaks from the heart.

MARY

When Lightfoot first began to discuss with Mr. Elijah Muhammad the idea of a public forum, it seemed like a marvelous idea. I knew he was distressed about the Muslim organization and felt a need to act. One of the many things that has made my husband a great man is his willingness, his drive to respond when he sees an individual or a situation that might benefit from his intervention.

But the debate did not go as we had anticipated. Some who were in the audience are calling my husband a "racial conservative." The Church of God has already lost some of its momentum due to Satan's work. Backlash from this event may have a negative impact on what we have worked so hard to build.

I'm concerned about Lightfoot's state of mind. Although he is not prone to depression, I sense discouragement. I hope I can find a way to comfort him.

Regretfully, part of my husband's motivation for arranging the debate was his frustration with that brother of his. Even after all these years, he was hopeful that Lewis would come back into the fold.

But the debate clearly did not have the desired effect. Lewis continues to hold Malcolm X in the highest esteem. And his relationship with Lightfoot is more strained than before. I think, finally, my husband has accepted the fact that his brother cannot be saved. The Word of God says, "He that hath ears to hear, let him hear." Everyone has ears, but not everyone can hear God. Perhaps now my husband will wash his hands of Lewis.

FBI FILES
1961

On September 7, 1961, LEWIS HENRI MICHAUX, owner of the National
Memorial African Bookstore, 2107 Seventh Avenue, New York City, attended a
mass rally for Unity, held at 125th Street and Seventh Avenue, sponsored by the
Emergency Committee for Unity on Social and Economic Problems (ECUSEP),
a newly formed committee representing most Negro groups in Harlem with its
purpose being to confront problems of racial violence.

A. Peter Bailey

All those black books! I've never seen anything like it. The Howard University bookstore had some black books but mainly textbooks. When I walked into Lewis Michaux's bookstore and saw all these histories, biographies and autobiographies, fliers and posters, it was mind-blowing.

And there's this big sign out front—*The House of Common Sense and the Home of Proper Propaganda.* It's a huge sign. I mean, you can read it from a block away. The store stands out. It just stands out.

I'm a reader and I've been a reader since I was a kid. No question, I'll be going back to that store. The place is a gold mine. I hear it's one of Malcolm X's hangouts. I can understand why.

Malcolm X (*center*) and Lewis Michaux (*right*)

NORRIS

Guess I was wrong about the bookstore. Lewis made it work. He really made it work. Don't ask me how, but that crazy s.o.b. got black people to buy books. White people too. And Afrocentric books. That's a bet I never would've taken. Never! Poppa would be dancing in the streets. There's nobody like Lewis. Nobody.

FBI FILES
1963

The *AMSTERDAM NEWS,* a daily newspaper published in Harlem, New York City, in its edition of March 9, 1963, published an article which appeared as follows:

"GHANAIAN CAPTAIN BRINGS SHIP HERE"

"Harlem and New York City had the enjoyable pleasure of viewing Ghana's steadily growing influence in winning friends, true and understandable to her role in world affairs for the future of Africa and African people.

"Dr. Kwame Nkrumah's Black Star Line Merchant Fleet Captain Tachie Menson mastered the 'Nasia River' into the port of New York Monday.

"Lewis H. Michaux, together with African nationals, were on hand to welcome the ship, officers, and crew. Mr. Michaux and African nationals presented Captain Tachie Menson with copies of a sketch depicting him as the inspirational reality of Marcus Garvey's dreams of 'black men sailing black-owned ships into ports of the world.'"

LEWIS

When I first met Kwame Nkrumah, he was still finding his way. Now he's president of Ghana and sending me gifts. It's nice to be remembered. Nkrumah's captain and crew brought me one hundred pounds of African coffee right from the Ivory Coast. Mmm, mmm. I'll keep it at the bookstore for sharing with select friends.

The coffee aside, it was gratifying to be standing on Nkrumah's Black Star Line Merchant ship, knowing it was a tribute to Garvey.

Lewis holds up a portrait of Nkrumah at a rally in 1960.

FBI FILES
1963

LEWIS H. MICHAUX, leader of the ANAI, a back-to-Africa black nationalist movement, attended a meeting of the ANAI, 2107 Seventh Avenue, New York City, on April 13, 1963, which was held at Seventh Avenue between 125th Street and 126th Street, New York City. Approximately one thousand Negro individuals were in attendance at this meeting during which many antiwhite statements were made.

The subject is owner of the National Memorial African Bookstore, 2107 Seventh Avenue, New York City. In November, 1961, MICHAUX founded and became the first president of the organization called Harlem African Black Nationalists. In June 1963, the Harlem African Black Nationalists were incorporated as African Nationals in America, Incorporated (ANAI). MICHAUX's bookstore sells antiwhite literature.

LEWIS

AUGUST 28 King is surely making an impact. Thousands of people gathered in D.C. today, and the entire nation watched him on television.

The man can talk, I'll say that. "I have a dream" was potent. Free at last? In an ideal world, maybe . . . but I'm a realist. King's dream, sadly, is just that. Real integration will never happen.

Martin Luther King Jr. delivers his "I have a dream" speech in Washington, D.C., on August 28, 1963.

Who should show up in the store today but Norris. Haven't seen him in a month of Sundays. He calls sometimes, but he doesn't get to Harlem much. He's still shooting pool but spends most of his free time at Rye Beach with Sinah and the grandkids.

So he walked in the store and, for a long time, just stood looking at the place. I could tell there was something on his mind. He wanted to speak but was having trouble finding the words. Then he said it. After all these years, Norris said, "I was wrong." I thought the sky was going to fall.

I didn't say I told you so. Just offered him a cup of my special African coffee.

Gus Travers
(OFF THE RECORD)

DECEMBER 2 Being a reporter has its perks. They weren't letting whites in the door. I only got in the rally because of my press pass. Otherwise, I wouldn't have heard him say it.

I know Malcolm X doesn't pull his punches, but what was he thinking? Less than a week after the president's funeral, he suggests Kennedy deserved it saying it was the "chickens coming home to roost."

Some people in the audience laughed. Others seemed to take it in stride, but the press pounced on it. A few reporters were fighting over a pay phone.

LEWIS

One day Malcolm says to me, "Michaux, this white man's got a lot to answer for."

"Well, Malcolm," I tell him, "you could say the chickens have finally come home to roost."

He took his notebook out and put that down. Last week, after President Kennedy was shot, he commented about the chickens coming home to roost. They jumped on him for that. They couldn't find nothin' else to say against him.

LEWIS

When Malcolm returned from his hajj, his pilgrimage to Mecca, he came to the bookstore.

"Dr. Michaux," he says. "I'm taking a new look at the old book."

"What old book?" I ask him.

"Mr. Muhammad teaches that no white people can become members of the Muslim movement," Malcolm said. "I went to Mecca and every nationality under the sun was there, and this proved to me that the present type of Islam that we have been taught here is just like black Christianity— segregated. And any religion, any man, that segregates because of color is out of order."

Elijah Muhammad was preaching a false setup. It was going under the heading of Muslim, but it wasn't the real thing.

Malcolm split with Elijah Muhammad because he wants to be a spokesman for black people period. Muhammad is only interested in you if you want to be a Muslim, and 80 percent of the so-called Negroes don't want no religion. They've had it with that. They want a program where they can survive, and Malcolm is saying "Whosoever will, let him come."

Christ, Himself, came to emancipate the common people, and the Bible says the common people heard Him gladly. Malcolm wants to be free, and he split with Mr. Muhammad so he won't have to toe a certain line. He can set up his own program and that's what he's doing. The Organization of Afro-American Unity. He's calling it—the OAAU. Anybody can join.

FBI FILES
1964

The *AMSTERDAM NEWS* edition of February 29, 1964, carried an article headlined, "Nationalist Pleads for Malcolm X," which stated "Harlem's Number One Black Nationalist This Week asks The Nation's Number One Black Muslim to deal lightly with Muslim Minister Malcolm X. The plea from Harlem was sent to Chicago by Lewis Henri MICHAUX, owner of a Negro bookstore at 125th Street and Seventh Avenue. He sent the message to Elijah Muhammad, Spiritual Leader of the Muslims, on the eve of the Black Muslim's Convention scheduled to be attended by thousands."

On March 26, 1964, MICHAUX attended a press conference held by Black Muslim Minister MALCOLM X at the Park Sheraton Hotel in New York City, at which time MALCOLM X announced he was leaving the Nation of Islam to form his own movement.

On June 3, 1964, MICHAUX attended a rally sponsored by the supporters of Malcolm X, which was held at the Audubon Ballroom, 166th Street and Broadway, New York City.

James E. Turner

I first saw Malcolm X at the bookstore where he comes to talk with Michaux. The corner outside the bookstore is a stage for street speakers in the tradition of Hyde Park in London and Union Square here in New York. Michaux, a major nationalist voice himself, introduces Malcolm at these rallies.

The more I listen, the more their analysis of our lack of power, our people having no sense of their history, those basic nationalist tenets—internal self-contempt, lack of ability to cooperate—begins to resonate.

Malcolm X speaks in front of the bookstore.

LEWIS

The other day, I gave Malcolm a check to help with the start-up of his new religious organization, the Muslim Mosque, Inc.

He says, "I thank Allah for this money."

I say, "Allah didn't give you that money. I gave you that money."

He laughs and says, "So, I thank you, Brother Michaux."

A. Peter Bailey

I've only been in Harlem two years, but those years have been life-changing. Meeting Brother Malcolm, finding Mr. Michaux's bookstore, and now getting involved in the Organization of Afro-American Unity.

At the meeting yesterday, when people were taking on jobs, no one offered to do the newsletter. Caught up in the moment, I volunteered. I've never done any journalistic writing. Never even wrote for my high school newspaper, and here I am, editor of the OAAU's paper, the *Blacklash.* I'll be learning as I go, but I'm up for it. I believe in this work and Brother Malcolm seems to have faith in me. He wants to bring *all* people of African descent together as a force for human rights. I guess he's starting with people like me.

I stop by the store at least once a week now. When I'm there, I don't just read. I listen. I listen to Brother Michaux talking about books and current events. He and his peers are like older brothers to the rest of us. They discuss issues and argue. I just stand around and get free history lessons.

Helen Brown, Bookstore Secretary

Lewis is correct. We have to get the word *Negro* out of our language. We have to stand up for our blackness.

Negroes are victims. Even if we see *ourselves* as black, we can't always control how others see us. I can say and believe that I'm a black woman, but if the man with the power sees me as a Negro, he treats me as a Negro—as a victim.

Since Lewis told me about getting twenty lashes for stealing a sack of peanuts as a boy, I can't seem to get it out of my mind—the look on his face, the humiliation, the resentment. This wound has never healed. But it surely didn't break his spirit. On the contrary, it fortified him.

Seems Lewis was *born* a black man. There was never any Negro in him. Our young people have to learn not to be victims. Many are getting it, and this bookstore is helping.

Bookstore Customer

FEBRUARY 21 Mr. Michaux edged his way through the crowd of us, all standing in front of the store. He seemed dazed.

Somebody said, "You were there, Professor. What happened?"

"I wasn't," Mr. Michaux said. He could hardly speak.

People started talking among themselves.

"Quiet now," I couldn't help saying. "Quiet." Everybody hushed and waited.

Finally, he began.

"I was to be on the platform with him at two o'clock to introduce his organization. I was about twenty-five minutes late because I had to go to Rockefeller Center to get my boy. He was skating down there." His eyes filled up.

After a moment, he continued.

"When I got to the Audubon, everybody was rushing out, screaming and hollering. I went inside and there he was, lying dead." Mr. Michaux shook his head. "I was supposed to be sitting beside him."

The bookstore had always been a noisy place with lots of talk. But the news of the murder left everyone without words. Most of us had heard

Malcolm speak right there out front. I felt the gratitude of having had the experience, and the sadness and bitterness of knowing that none of us would ever hear Malcolm again.

NEW YORK REGISTER
FEBRUARY 22, 1965

MALCOLM X MURDERED IN HARLEM
FOLLOWERS SHARE FRUSTRATION AND SORROW

BY GUS TRAVERS

Black nationalist Malcolm X was killed at the Audubon Ballroom where he was scheduled to speak yesterday on behalf of his Organization of Afro-American Unity. As he stood at the lectern, a loud argument distracted the crowd of onlookers, and a man armed with a shotgun rushed the stage and fired twice, fatally wounding the former Nation of Islam member.

Weeks before Malcolm X was to speak, he ordered an end to security checks of those who would be entering the hall.

"If I can't be safe among my own kind," he said, "where can I be?"

Despite the Valentine's Day firebombing of his home, he attended today's rally as scheduled. Those closest to him said he seemed unusually anxious when he arrived at the ballroom—almost as if he knew his days were numbered.

During the first seconds of his address before four hundred attendees, the threats on his life were carried out. Three alleged members of the Nation of Islam (NOI), one armed with a 12-gauge shotgun, the others with handguns, stood and opened fire, sending bullets ripping through the controversial black leader.

Malcolm X was pronounced dead on arrival at the nearby Vanderbilt Clinic Medical Center. He was thirty-nine years old.

The feud between Malcolm X and Elijah Muhammad and the Nation of Islam is well known. Talk of revenge by many of the murdered leader's followers, who suspect Muhammad orchestrated the assassination, led police last night to bring three hundred additional officers from Brooklyn, Queens, and the Bronx to keep the peace in Harlem. There were no incidents of public unrest.

Many Malcolm X supporters gathered outside the Hotel Theresa, where the black leader kept an office. Others convened across the street in front of the National

Memorial African Bookstore, where the self-described human rights advocate often led rallies or consulted with the store's owner, Lewis Michaux. But there was no further display of violence—only talk of the tragedy and Malcolm X's legacy.

One man outside of the bookstore said, "Malcolm spoke up for the people. He was doing what he thought was right. Any time leaders speak for the people they are killed."

"Why wasn't he protected?" asked a man dressed in a suit and tie. "The handwriting was on the wall."

"We all know who wanted him dead, but there won't be any justice because the power elite doesn't care. They're glad that somebody else got rid of Malcolm so they won't have to," added a young man dressed entirely in black.

A passerby commented, "Isn't he the one who said the chickens have come home to roost? Well now he knows what that's like."

Tears streaked the face of a woman holding a sign that read: "He didn't die in vain."

Outspoken bookstore owner, Lewis Michaux, was uncharacteristically silent.

Followers and audience members attend to the fatally wounded Malcolm X.

BETTIE

FEBRUARY 22 New York City police officers came to the house to question Lewis about Malcolm's murder. With Lewis Jr.—just nine years old—standing right there. Can you imagine?

I brought him right into the kitchen and turned up the radio.

LEWIS JR.

FEBRUARY 22 I'm sad those men killed Mr. Malcolm, but I'm glad my dad is all right. I'm glad I went skating and Dad came to get me. I'm glad.

Gus Travers,
New York City Newspaper Reporter
(OFF THE RECORD)

FEBRUARY Up in Harlem today, I see Michaux's been composing again. There's a new sign outside his bookstore:

> MAN, IF YOU THINK BRO. MALCOLM IS DEAD,
> YOU ARE OUT OF YOUR COTTON PICKING HEAD.
> JUST GET UP OFF YOUR SLUMBERING BED,
> AND WATCH HIS FIGHTING SPIRIT SPREAD.
> EVERY SHUT EYE AIN'T SLEEP.
> EVERY GOOD-BYE AIN'T GONE.

Inside, Michaux is at work, sharing books, talking with customers as usual. But something's missing. That spring in his step. That energy.

He's mourning.

LEWIS

They had to get rid of Malcolm because he was rocking the boat. Malcolm was the freest man.

The Nation of Islam did a lot for him, but you can't hog-tie a man's knowledge. After training a man to do a thing, sometimes the student is better than the teacher. What happened was jealousy. All the press and everybody wanted to talk with Malcolm, not old Elijah Muhammad, 'cause Muhammad can't talk, can't entertain an audience. Malcolm kept an audience spellbound.

Malcolm is reincarnated in the minds and spirits of our young people. Garvey woke 'em up. And Malcolm got 'em up. When a man tells the truth, a lot of people claim he's stirring something up. But if the truth stirs it up, let it come! Let it come!

A. Peter Bailey

I remember when I first heard Brother Malcolm.

I moved to Harlem on a Friday night the summer of '62. Saturday afternoon I walked along Lenox Avenue, just to look around. I got up to 116th Street and saw a crowd gathering. Someone said Malcolm X was going to speak. What little I'd heard had made him out to be a bogeyman, so I was curious.

When Brother Malcolm spoke, he always quoted books and articles, and made you want to go get the books and read those articles. That's how I started going to the bookstore. Mr. Michaux was Malcolm's master teacher. Brother Malcolm would go there, and from what I understand, he would get into those books and Brother Michaux would just close up the shop and leave him in there. What Malcolm learned from him, he would impart to us. So there was that link. The store was one of Brother Malcolm's major learning places, especially when it came to history. And he would speak there at the space in front of the store. They would set the ladders out, and he would climb up and speak.

That's all gone now. I was in the Audubon Ballroom when it happened. I don't know what to do with the feelings. Anger . . . frustration . . . grief. It's too much. I need to get away from here for a while. Maybe after the funeral.

Rodnell Collins

I wasn't surprised to see Brother Michaux at the funeral. He was a major influence and source of support for my uncle, very much like a father to him.

His National Memorial African Bookstore provided an important part of Uncle Malcolm's social, philosophical, and psychological diet. It was not an ordinary bookstore, but part library and part school. Brother Michaux had seemingly endless energy and was an expert on the Harlem Renaissance.

When visiting Uncle Malcolm, Ma and I would meet him at the store, where he was welcomed any time of day or night. He spent more time there than anywhere else in New York City. I believe, at times, Malcolm may have actually lived there. Sometimes he would fall asleep while reading in the back room. Brother Michaux would usually have a pile of phone messages or mail for Malcolm when he stopped by, since people who wanted to contact him would phone or write the store.

There were occasions when Ma, Uncle Malcolm, and Brother Michaux would talk all night while I slept peacefully among a cavern of books. Malcolm loved books with a passion. He seemed to be in seventh heaven when in the store or in the basement of his own home, where books abounded—on the floor, on shelves on the walls, on tables and desks.

It was at Brother Michaux's in the 1950s that Ma and I first really saw and felt for ourselves how a crowd in an outdoor space was affected by my uncle's words, feelings, and convictions. We had always seen him speak in a temple, inside public arenas, and in television or radio studios. When we saw him speak outdoors in front of the bookstore, in the open air, with or without a microphone, he never missed a beat, speaking clearly, bluntly, passionately, and accurately about the racial reality in this country. His words of wisdom would inspire crowds of hundreds, sometimes thousands of people. I had no idea he could touch people like that. Even a person who disliked or hated what he said would be impressed by his oratorical skills.

This is why they feared him. This is why they murdered him.

LEWIS

Malcolm never spoke on the platform until after he came in and got his notes together in the back of the store. Thousands of people would be outside waiting, but his bodyguards would escort him inside, and we would sit down and talk about different things. We'd laugh and joke and talk serious.

I miss that. Our conversations.

I got more mail for him at the store today. Guess I'll walk it on over to his sister, Ella, at the OAAU office.

Malcolm X at the bookstore in 1964

FBI FILES
1966

MICHAUX attended a memorial for MALCOLM X on February 21, 1966, which was held at 178 West 135th Street, New York City.

ONLY A TREE WILL STAND STILL WHILE IT'S BEING CHOPPED DOWN.

White College Professor

When I took my students to Harlem last week, it was with the arrogant notion of giving them a ghetto experience, one they could not gain in the classroom. It went pretty much as expected, until we found the National Memorial African Bookstore and Lewis Michaux.

I have visited with many respected scholars all over the country about the question of race, but after listening to him in the tiny, dusty, overstuffed back room at his bookstore, I discover I haven't been anywhere.

Our interview with Michaux was memorable. Indeed, the students were somewhat unsettled over the way he outlined the conditions of black people and the reasons they are in this predicament.

His words were stinging.

"You white people . . ."

I almost ended the discussion right then but held off. There was a compelling intensity in his voice.

". . . have been throwing us out of the window and thought we were gone," he said, "like a man who lives in a castle and keeps on throwing bones and bread crumbs out the window and then sees those things come back to him in the form of roaches. Now what you've done is pushed us and pushed us back into these ghettos and thought we would stay there. But we've come out of the ghetto. We're in Times Square and out in your neighborhood in Westchester. We've spread everywhere. The ghetto can't hold us. You created this. You're responsible."

Stinging, yes, but thought provoking.

One student asked, "What can we do to help, Mr. Michaux?"

He said, "Some men came to me the other day and asked the same question. I said, 'You want to help the ghetto? Go home and pull off those fancy clothes, put on an apron and get you a broom and go down in the community and help those people clean up their houses and you'll prove to them that you're sincere.' People always want to know what can *we* do? But it isn't what '*we* do,' but what you do as an individual."

LEWIS

My father said to me when I was a child, "Boy, set there until I come back." That was his law and I had to obey him. He went off somewhere and forgot about me. I sat there all day waiting for my father and almost got a stroke from the sun.

I said to my son one time, "Boy, set there until I come back." You know what he said to me? "For what?"

You're not going to cram down the throats of today's youth what got crammed down my father's. Young people want to know the facts now. We need institutions like this bookstore so the kids can educate themselves.

Snooze

Yesterday I go into the bookstore and give The Professor the closed-fist salute.

"What's that?" he asks.

"Black Power!" I reply. *Cool.*

"Where'd you learn that?" Mr. Michaux asks.

"The brothers in the Movement," I say.

"Open your hand," Mr. Michaux says.

I do.

"See, you ain't got nothing in it."

He picks up a book, puts it in my hand, and says, "Now that's power! Tell your brothers in the Movement that black is beautiful, but knowledge is power."

Black Panthers *(left to right)* Stokely Carmichael, LeRoi Jones, and H. Rap Brown at the store

LEWIS

I remember the day that banker refused me a loan because "Negroes don't read." Back then, I couldn't make enough money to pay the light bill. Now it's wonderful to walk in this store and hear, "That's $32.70 plus tax." That's one person! All day long this is going on. Sometimes, I can't hardly get in this store for all the people. And today young people come in here at times buying four and five books. I mean *little* kids eight and nine years old.

Every company that publishes books on black people sends me copies now. I've gotten letters from writers and editors saying I'm responsible for opening up the avenue of publishers accepting black manuscripts.

And some of the books here in the store are collector's items. I've made it my business to find out-of-print books, if they can be found. I've built up my reputation and people are saying, "If you can't find it at Michaux's, don't look no more." It pays to be sincere in what you're doing.

True, I haven't been to a show or a movie but once in thirty years. I don't go hardly anywhere 'cept here and home. When I'm home, I read. I stick to my business. I've found out that if you want a crop to grow, you tend it. Any woman who has a baby and don't give it plenty of her milk and she goes and leaves it with somebody else to nurse, that woman's in for a mess when she comes back to get that baby. Well, I nursed this business and it's grown up nicely.

A fellow told me one day, "I guess you're doing well enough now to move into one of those upper-class neighborhoods."

Sure, I could move. But I won't. Sometimes I go up on the mountain and it's nice up there. But I made it in the valley, so I got to come back to the valley to live. I love Harlem and wouldn't move out of here for nothing.

Street Hustler

The Professor? Yeah, he's cool. Me and my boys, we hit some other places around Harlem, but the bookstore—that's off-limits. We scratch each others' backs, if you get my meaning. He helps us out when we need it, and we keep an eye on the store for him. 'Cause there's some bad people out there. The Prof knows all he needs to do is blow his bugle and we'll bring the cavalry.

LEWIS

No dope addicts come in here and stick me up. They protect me.

They come in here sometimes and say, "Professor, give me fifty cents. I want to go downtown."

I put out about thirty-five dollars a month giving fifty cents and quarters. They wouldn't let nobody roll this store. If there's a disturbance of any kind, you'll see 'em rush in here and say, "What's the matter, Professor? Need me?"

I say "Naw, everything's cool."

LEWIS

To say Mary and I didn't harmonize on much is an understatement. Still, I'm sorry for her passing. I feel for Lightfoot. He's hurting. Sixty years is a long time for two people to live together as man and wife. On the other hand, this is the day she's been living for since she found her religion.

No question, Mary and I were day and night. But I guess I should thank her for all the times she prayed for my soul. Not many people do. Maybe I should worry there's one less around.

I give the woman credit. She set her mind to saving souls and put everything she had into it. Like that Young People's Purity Club she started. "Be a Peach Out of Reach," she told the ladies. And "If there is nothing for sale, take the sign down." That Mary was something. Firm, relentless in her teaching of high—if she was living, I'd say high and mighty—morals and virtuous living to young people. As tiresome as she was, Mary was fixed, certain, unchanging in her beliefs. I tip my hat to her on that. I might even find myself missing her flak.

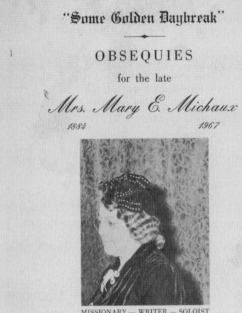

"Some Golden Daybreak"

OBSEQUIES

for the late

Mrs. Mary E. Michaux
1884   1967

MISSIONARY — WRITER — SOLOIST

Devoted wife of

ELDER LIGHTFOOT SOLOMON MICHAUX

Sunday, November 5, 1967
11:00 o'clock a.m.
at the
CHURCH OF GOD
19th Street and Jefferson Avenue
Newport News, Virginia

Arrangements by the Johnson and Jenkins Funeral Home
4804 Georgia Avenue, N.W. Washington, D. C.

Funeral service program for Mary Michaux

Poet Nikki Giovanni

When *Black Feeling, Black Talk* came out last month, Lewis was kind enough to put it in his store. I was thrilled. If you're a black writer, there are three places you want to carry your books—Curtis Ellis in Chicago, Marcus Books in San Francisco, and Michaux's in New York. Michaux, of course, is the pioneer.

I visit Michaux's a couple of times a week, and yesterday, when I walked in, Lewis said, "Nikki . . ." Actually, he calls me Giovanni. He said, "Giovanni, guess what?"

I said, "What?"

He said, "Your book was stolen."

I said, "Oh!" thinking this was a bad thing.

But he said, "That's wonderful! People want to read you!"

I laughed.

If Lewis is happy about this, maybe I'll have a career.

BROADSIDE PRESS: Detroit. $1.00

Nikki Giovanni

BLACK FEELING

BLACK TALK

Cover of Nikki Giovanni's first poetry collection

LEWIS

When I get the news that Cleaver is coming to town, I want him to autograph his book at the store.

So I call the publisher and say, "I want five hundred copies of Cleaver's book, *Soul on Ice.* He's in town and I want him to autograph it."

The man says, "Do you have an account with us?"

I've been purchasing most of my books from jobbers, so I often don't buy directly from publishers.

"No, I haven't," I say. "But I've got to have them in the morning."

The man says, "It's impossible for you to get them by tomorrow morning because you have to establish your credit. I'll have to send you an application."

"But Cleaver will be here tomorrow. I've got to have the books," I tell him.

Eldridge Cleaver, 1968

"Wait a minute," he says and calls another man to the phone.

"Who is this?" the second man asks. "Are you the man who's been up on Seventh Avenue for years selling Negro books?"

"That's me."

And the man says, "The books will be there in the morning."

And here they are. Right on time.

The House of Common Sense is getting some respect.

Nikki Giovanni

Well, I have arrived! Lewis invited me in for a cup of coffee, and I'm not talking Chock full o'Nuts. I'm talking about his African coffee from Nkrumah. *The* coffee from Ghana's Black Star Line.

When he closed the store tonight, Lewis looked at me and said, "Giovanni, would you like a cup of coffee?" I knew what he meant, and I know you have to be pretty important to be asked.

So here I sit in the National Memorial African Bookstore, talking with Lewis, sipping his coffee, savoring the moment, making it last.

Yes, I have arrived.

LEWIS JR.

APRIL 4 After I heard the news, I headed for Seventh Avenue. It was scary on 125th, but I needed to see Mom and Dad. When black folks heard Dr. King was killed, they went wild. Throwing rocks and burning things. Breaking windows. Taking stuff from stores. Some people were just running the streets screaming and crying. When I got to the bookstore, Mom was getting ready to close up.

"Child, what in the world are you doing here? Didn't I tell you to stay home?" She pulled me in and locked the door.

Dad hugged me and said, "We lost another one, son."

I went to look out the window, but Mom pulled me back.

"You get away from there! What is wrong with you?"

Dad sat down and put his head in his hands.

"It's senseless," he said.

Looters got into the jeweler's next door, the butcher's, and about every other store around us. But they didn't bother our place. They didn't touch the bookstore.

LEWIS

APRIL 5 I didn't always agree with King, but he surely did his part as a soldier in the fight for right.

Some think if they can eliminate the outspoken among us, black people will crawl away defeated. But they're wrong. Others will find their voices, sharpen their weapons, join the battle.

I am not a violent man. I fight my battles with words, but I understand why so many black people are angry.

Violence originated in Heaven, and God used it on His enemy the Devil. He threw him the hell out of Heaven, and that's violence. And all through the Old Testament, God advocated violence. If it was good for Him, it's good for me when the time comes. In Ecclesiastes, Solomon says there's a season and a time for every purpose under the sun. A time to get and a time to lose. A time to love, to hate, to kill, to be born, to embrace your wife, to turn her loose. And there's a time to use violence. If God uses it, and He's perfect, man has a perfect right to use it when he's attacked.

Sometimes a man gets pushed, pushed too hard. Too far.

Until the neglected and the rejected are accepted and respected, there's gonna be no damn peace . . . nowhere! Only a tree will stand still while it's being chopped down.

SECTION 7
1968–1976

WE'RE GOING TO CALL IT A DAY.

FBI FILES
1968

Lewis MICHAUX, owner of the National Memorial African Bookstore, planned
to start a protest movement against the New York state government because
of the plans for a state building on West 125th Street, Harlem. MICHAUX
believes that the erection of this building at this location is an attempt by the
government to eliminate his bookstore, which has become a rallying point for
Black Nationalists.

BETTIE

When Lewis learned New York had bought four city blocks to build a state office building in Harlem, he wasn't concerned. He wasn't worried even when he learned that our bookstore stands on one of those blocks. And when some local people approached him to sign a petition protesting the state tearing up the black community, Lewis wouldn't sign it.

"Most of these businesses are not black owned anyway," he said. "Who am I to stand in the way of progress?"

He told me later that new construction could be a good thing for Harlem; it would bring business to the area.

More than that, Lewis had a meeting with Governor Nelson Rockefeller to discuss the matter. He felt confident he and the governor could come to some kind of agreement.

When Governor Rockefeller visited the bookstore, he asked, "Are all these books about black people?"

He was impressed, but he quickly got to the point. He told Lewis we would have to move the store.

"I'm not against the state building, and I'm not against progress," Lewis told him, "but I want you to remember me and this place."

Rockefeller said, "We'll remember you."

Two days later we got the keys to a storefront at 125th Street and Lenox Avenue, a few blocks down from where we are now. The governor told Lewis we can stay there until the state building is finished and that we will have a place on the new site.

Lewis is banking on the governor's promise.

Gus Travers,
New York City Newspaper Reporter
(OFF THE RECORD)

Harlem is no longer my beat, but I remember the first time this reporter was sent to cover the National Memorial African Bookstore and Lewis Michaux. Not your average story. Not your average man. Over the years, I developed an affection for Michaux. On a slow news day, I could often count on him to provide me with great material, along with some laughs.

Now I hear he's being forced to relocate down 125th Street from Seventh to Lenox, a move which will certainly disrupt the store's functioning and could jeopardize its future.

The question on the street is was there a political agenda in selecting Harlem Square for the new state building? Is the white power structure so fearful of the bookstore's activities that it will go to any lengths to stifle them?

You've been living in a cave if you have to ask.

No question which side this reporter is on.

Snooze

The Man is always pushing us around, politicians taking whatever they want.

When I heard they were forcing Mr. Michaux to move, I thought, that's it, I'm ready to start picketing at that office building site.

So when the store reopened today, I hoof it on up there to check it out.

It's good to see so many old customers. And there's a new sign above his door: *Knowledge is power—you need it every hour. Read a Book.*

The Professor is still getting the message out, so things haven't changed that much. College is back in session. I hope there's something new from James Baldwin.

LEWIS

Moving was hell, but it gave us an opportunity to do a real inventory of our stock. Over two hundred thousand books. A far cry from the five I started with.

Rent is higher, but we're managing. The regulars are finding their way here, so it seems to be business as usual.

Willie Stone

I've been looking for something—a direction? an identity? When I mention this to one of the brothers at the Black Panther meeting, he tells me about the National Memorial African Bookstore in Harlem. So I go there and meet Mr. Michaux, this feisty little man they call The Professor.

I tell him, "I'm learning how to get away from being a Negro. I'm looking for books about the African. Books that will teach me how to be a better black man."

"How to be a better black man?" he says. "Brother, you don't learn how to be black from no damn book. I don't care who wrote it. There isn't one book in this store that can give you any soul. Soul is something that, if you are not born with it, forget it. So, young brother, that is your answer for getting your blackness from a book. You have to live, breathe, and *be* black to have blackness."

I look at the hundreds of books. It didn't make sense. Wasn't he going to let me read even one lousy book?

Then his voice gentled down. "Brother, if you are already a true black person, then books will help you pick a better path and program. They can give you the knowledge of the failure of others. They can give you guidance for success in being black."

Mr. Michaux takes me to a little room in the back. It is cluttered with African artifacts, letters and pictures of famous blacks. Beautiful hand-carved African objects adorn the walls. Letters from George Washington Carver, Marian Anderson, and many other famous blacks hang on the wall. I know now I am in more than just a bookstore.

I had intended to go to the store, maybe find one book, and leave. Instead, I stay all morning, lost in the culture surrounding me, and listening to conversation about black issues and heritage.

Before I leave, I ask Mr. Michaux to recommend some books for me to read. He picks five, saying, "You bring these books back and I'm going to ask you questions. If you've read and understood the books, they'll cost you nothing. If you can't answer the questions correctly, you're going to pay full price. Fair enough?"

"Yes, sir!" I say before thinking about how I'll pay for the books if I flunk his test.

As I walk down 125th Street, I say to myself, "There's no more Negro in me. There's nothing but pure blackness."

FBI FILES
JUNE 1968

Title of Case:

Louis Michaux, aka

Louis H. Michaux

Lewis Henry Michaux

Lewis Henri Michaux

Lewis H. Michaux

Lewis Michaux

RACIAL MATTERS

During the month of May 1968, informants familiar with racial activity in the NYC area were contacted relative to MICHAUX's connection with black nationalist activities in Harlem, NYC area. Sources advised they could furnish no pertinent information concerning subject's involvement with any black nationalist activities nor the printing of antiwhite literature at the present time.

Case is being placed in a closed status as information received failed to show subject as being currently active in black nationalist activities or with any black militant organization. Subject is therefore not being recommended for placement on the Security Index and/or the Rabble Rouser Index.

In the event information is received showing subject to be active in black militant activities, then case will be reopened.

LEWIS

WASHINGTON, D.C. Seeing Brother in that hospital bed shook me. I'd never seen Lightfoot so vulnerable. This is a man who was always in charge. *He* held the reins. *He* wore the crown. But lying in that bed, he looked small. Feeble. Broken. I guess we're all so busy living our lives that we don't notice when age creeps up on us.

Lightfoot and I had our differences. We've taken paths that usually led us to places the other couldn't go without losing himself. I'm okay with that. And I think on some level, Brother understood this too. We have that much respect for each other.

Mother always knew her favorite child would do great things. And Poppa, well, he would have his chest puffed out at what Lightfoot has accomplished.

NEGRO RELIGIOUS LEADER DIES AT 84

WASHINGTON, D.C., October 20, Elder Lightfoot Solomon Michaux, charismatic Negro founder of the Church of God, died at Freedman's Hospital today at the age of eighty-four. He had suffered a stroke in August.

Known as the "Happy Am I" evangelist, Elder Michaux conducted his first church service in 1917 under a tent in his hometown of Newport News, Virginia, before a congregation of 150 people. He went on to establish seven churches. Elder Michaux, his choir and his theme song, "Happy Am I," gained international attention through radio broadcasts, which began at WTOP in Washington in the early 1930s. The programs were picked up by the Columbia Broadcasting System and the British Broadcasting Company. His services later were aired on television station WTTG in Washington.

"Happy Am I"

OBSEQUIES

for the late

Elder Lightfoot Solomon Michaux

Sunday, October 27, 1968
11:00 o'clock a.m.

at the

CHURCH OF GOD
19th Street and Jefferson Avenue
Newport News, Virginia

Arrangements by the Johnson and Jenkins Funeral Home
4804 Georgia Avenue, N.W.   Washington, D. C.

Funeral service program for Lightfoot

After establishing his Washington, D.C., church under the Gospel Spreading Association in 1928, Elder Michaux's fame was heightened by his dynamic marches and baptismal services featuring his "Cross Choir" of 156 trained singers. He baptized followers in the Potomac River and, later, at Griffith Stadium where he drew crowds as large as 25,000 people. Attracting both Negro and white followers to his ministry, Michaux was once arrested for holding racially integrated baptismal services.

Elder Michaux established a monthly church publication, *Happy News*; an employment agency for church and community members; a housing development for Negroes; and the Happy News Cafe, a lunchroom which fed people in need.

Elder Michaux was a friend and political associate of President Franklin Delano Roosevelt, who admired the minister for his charitable work on behalf of Negroes during the Depression. Elder Michaux was also on close terms with FBI Director J. Edgar Hoover and President Harry S. Truman. President Dwight D. Eisenhower was an honorary deacon of the Washington Church of God.

The son of a seafood merchant, Elder Michaux worked in his father's business in Newport News before entering the ministry.

Survivors include three sisters, Ruth Michaux (Washington, D.C.), Margaret Banks (New York, NY), and Jennie MacRae (Newport News, VA); and two brothers, Lewis Michaux (New York, NY) and Norris Michaux (Port Chester, NY).

Funeral arrangements are not finalized, but services will take place at the Church of God in Newport News, Virginia. Elder Michaux will be buried next to his wife, Mary, at Pleasant Shade Cemetery, near the church.

FBI FILES
NOVEMBER 1968

By means of a suitable pretext conducted by a Special Agent (SA) of the Federal Bureau of Investigation, November 5, 1968.

NATIONAL MEMORIAL AFRICAN BOOKSTORE, NEW YORK CITY

A confidential source of the New York Office advised that the National Memorial African Bookstore is operated by Lewis MICHAUX. MICHAUX originally set up the bookstore at 2107 Seventh Avenue, New York City. The current location for the bookstore is 101 West 125th Street, New York City. The store retails books both fiction and nonfiction, specializing in those about the Negro race.

A source advised the National Memorial African Bookstore does not publish or print books, but only sells them. Many of the books are of black nationalist theme such as can be purchased in drugstores and other business establishments in the Negro areas of New York City.

The same confidential source advised that the National Memorial African Bookstore is not a gathering place for black nationalists, although various Harlem leaders have been seen purchasing books at the bookstore. There are no newspapers or periodicals of black extremist organizations for sale. Lewis MICHAUX seems to be semiretired and is definitely not an active black nationalist leader at this time. Those books observed for sale appeared to be published by nationally known publishing houses. MICHAUX has not been known to make any violent statements, or to encourage violence.

LEWIS

Lightfoot often began his sermons with, "My precious ones . . ."

Seems I'm not among his chosen.

I understand why Lightfoot cut me out of his will. We had our differences. He included me in the 1953 and the 1958 versions but gave my portion to Willie in the 1966 version. She's been loyal to him and the church all these years.

Because Mary died before Lightfoot, the court named me executor. I want to see the family through this, but now a fourth will has turned up— supposedly written in 1968—that leaves everything to the Church.

I don't believe it. If my brother wanted them Negroes to have the money, he'd'a left them the money.

(o) ONE SIXTH ~~TO MY BROTHER LOUIS MICHAUX~~ *L.S. Michaux*

IN MONTHLY INSTALLMENTS DURING THE REMAINDER OF ~~HIS~~ *her* LIFE *L.S. Michaux*

~~AND UPON HIS DEATH SAID PAYMENTS~~ TO BE MADE MONTHLY TO ~~MRS~~ *my*

to my sister-in-law
~~MRS~~ WILLIA ANN MICHAUX FOR THE REMAINDER OF HER LIFE.

UPON HER DEATH TO DIVIDE THE THEN PRINCIPAL OF THE TRUST

IN ONE-TWELFTH EQUAL PART WHICH SHALL BE GIVEN ABSOLUTELY

Excerpt from Lightfoot's will showing Lightfoot's note to remove Lewis's name

Lewis at the store in the late 1960s

Charles E. Becknell

I'd just finished reading *Before the Mayflower* as part of my fellowship work at Columbia University. A powerful book. I've always been interested in black history, but this course fueled something new in me.

I figured the Schomburg library was the place to go in New York for black history research, so I asked one of my professors how to get there.

"Yes," he said, "but I think you also need to go to Michaux's bookstore in Harlem."

He told me where to find it, and I walked across campus, through Morningside Park, and down to the bookstore.

I introduced myself to Mr. Michaux and asked about John Hope Franklin's *From Slavery to Freedom*. He directed me right to it. He seemed to have material on anything I asked about and some comment or piece of information to share.

I've been spending a lot of my free time in Mr. Michaux's bookstore. Yesterday, there was a man speaking, standing on a ladder on the street corner, and people were gathering around. I thought, "The guy's nuts."

I asked somebody, "Who is he?"

The man said, "His name is Charles Kenyatta."

I said, "That name sounds familiar."

He said, "Yeah, he was one of the lieutenants for Malcolm X."

I stayed around and listened. And learned.

I *did* make it to the Schomburg library just so I could say I've been there, but everything I need is right at Mr. Michaux's bookstore.

BETTIE

I'm worried about Lewis. Ever since Lightfoot's passing, he hasn't been the same. The spark, the lightness in his walk, is absent. The brothers had their conflicts, but their inner bond was never broken. Lewis feels this loss deeply.

And just as he was starting to recover from relocating the store, the fiasco with the will began.

First, we learned Lightfoot had disinherited Lewis. I wasn't really surprised, knowing how offended Elder was by Lewis's friendship with Malcolm. I suppose when Lightfoot finally accepted the fact there was nothing he could do to influence this alliance and realized he would never be able to rein Lewis back in to the Church, he gave up on his brother. Elder would say it was business. Church business. He surely had difficulty with anyone he could not control. So the disinheritance was no bolt from the blue.

But now, as executor, Lewis is having to deal with multiple wills and the Church, the bank, the lawyers, and the family, all staking claims.

My husband is pushing eighty. Keeping the store going *and* those trips to Washington for meetings about the estate are just too much for him. For me, as well. I do my best to run the business while he's away, but I'm no spring chicken myself.

1973

LEWIS

I was depending on Governor Rockefeller, but since the Rock left office, things have changed. They want me out so they can tear down this building. I just want to stay where I am until they finish the project.

The higher-ups still insist there will be a place for the bookstore on the east side of the state office building. I want to believe them, but my faith is failing. And so is my spirit.

I'm getting old. Tired.

BETTIE

AUTUMN Lewis received an eviction order today from the State of New York. We have to vacate the premises by January 1. This time, there's no place to go. We understood there was no room for commercial businesses in the state building. But the eastern portion of the site was to house cultural, educational, and commercial facilities. It was our understanding that the bookstore would be in this eastern section. Now it appears there will *be* no eastern section.

Rockefeller's promise was empty. Though he's no longer governor, Lewis has left messages for him, but there's been no response. Governor Wilson has remained silent on the matter. I doubt state officials ever really intended to keep Rockefeller's promise. It wouldn't surprise me if relocation was just the first step in putting us out of business.

Lewis is discouraged.

I'm angry.

JET MAGAZINE
FEBRUARY 7, 1974

EVICTION OF HARLEM BOOKSTORE OWNER IS PROTESTED BY LEADERS

Harlemites are rallying by the hundreds around Lewis H. Michaux, owner of the National Memorial African Bookstore, to protest a state eviction order that would remove the bookstore from its 125th Street location in the heart of Harlem.

In 1968, Michaux vacated his original location further up the block on Seventh Avenue to make way for the new state office building, and moved to his present location. According to Michaux, former Gov. Nelson A. Rockefeller told him: "We're going to leave that building at the present site until the state office building is completed."

Then, last fall, Michaux received the state eviction order effective January 1 of this year, but he could not find suitable space to house his large collection of books. According to his latest inventory, "we have more than 225,000 books, particularly on black people," Michaux said.

The Memorial Bookstore is also a kind of shrine for serious students of black life and culture. In addition to his collection of books, Michaux has photographs, paintings and mementos of leaders of African countries of the post-colonial period.

The building that houses the bookstore is the last remaining edifice on the site being cleared for the eastern portion of the state office building projected to house cultural, educational and commercial facilities. If all goes well, the future site of the bookstore will be in the eastern part. But in the interim, Michaux and his supporters do not want the Harlem community to be deprived of the Memorial Bookstore for any period of time.

Harlem Hustler

When we heard the Man was messing with him we told The Professor we could help.

I said, "Just say the word, Prof. We'll burn down that new state building. Let those mothers know they're jerking the wrong people around."

The Professor smiled but shook his head, "That's no way to hold a discussion."

I could tell he thought about it though.

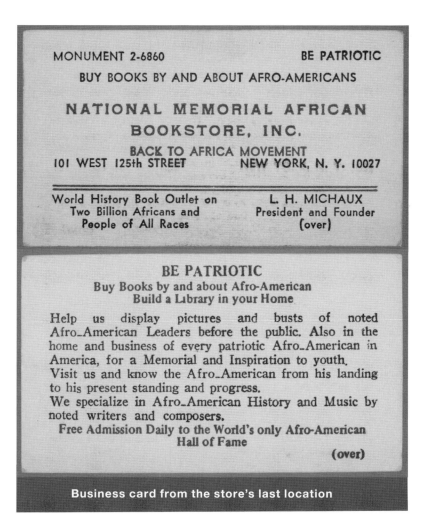

Business card from the store's last location

LEWIS

When bad things happen, you find out who your friends are. Seems I have many, and they've been raising hell all over the place about this eviction. I'm grateful. The protests may have bought us more time, but I know the reality.

Even if the state gives us a location, I'm getting too old to run things. The bookstore is my baby, but it's gotten too heavy for me. And Bettie's made it clear that when I retire, she'll be ready too. I don't blame her. She's worked like a dog right next to me. If there's a heaven, that's where she's going.

Lewis Jr. is at Ithaca. His mind is on basketball and women, as it should be. He's a nineteen-year-old college kid. Not that he doesn't care about the store. I know he does. But bookselling is *my* passion, not his.

I doubt I can find a buyer. The uncertainty of the location is a gamble investors won't bet on. I wouldn't. As a young man, maybe, but not anymore.

Now I know how Poppa must have felt. He spent his whole life building a business and died knowing it would die with him.

The days of the National Memorial African Bookstore are numbered. It looks like mine are too. You'd think those sore throats I've been having this past year would have tipped me off. Should have gone to see a doctor back then, but I figured I'd go, give him my money, and he'd look in my throat and say, "Here, take some cough medicine and go to bed." I can do that myself for free. And who's had time, with the eviction. And Brother's estate. Even if I'd seen a doctor, would it have mattered? By the time I felt the symptoms, the cancer had already found its home in my throat.

I guess I could blame it on cigarettes. But the truth is, nobody made me smoke 'em. Well . . . nature produces you and nature reduces you. I'm bucking against nature now. Nature has told me to sit down before I fall down. But I want to die on the battlefield.

Gus Travers, New York City Newspaper Reporter
(OFF THE RECORD)

When I first saw the ad, I'd hoped Michaux was just trying to reduce stock, so there'd be fewer books to put in storage until he could reopen at a new site. But it's clear he's going out of business. The last paragraph of the ad clinched it: "We're going to call it a day . . ."

He would have been retiring soon anyway, I imagine. But it's a sad day for the neighborhood. Harlem has lost part of its social consciousness.

NEW YORK AMSTERDAM NEWS

OCTOBER 26, 1974

National Memorial African Bookstore, Inc.

101 West 125th Street, New York, NY 10027

Special SALE Notice

TO THE PEOPLE OF HARLEM

From the National Memorial African Bookstore

The oldest Black Bookstore in the U.S.A. with the largest collection of books by and about Black people in the world, regrets to announce that after 35 years of serving the Harlem community as a branch of the learning tree of knowledge, we are being forced to move from our present location at 101 West 125th Street, to make room for the completion of the State Project.

We are currently running an anniversary sale which will continue throughout the months of November and December. We have 20,000 Black books which are regularly priced from $3.00-$10.00, however, during our sale they will sell for 99 cents each. We also have 50,000 current Black publications which are being sold for 1/2 the regular list price. There are hundreds of children's books included in these collections. Of special interest to the parents of Harlem, we have 20,000 paperbound books giving the history, in pictures, of how the children of Africa live. These books will be given away to every child between the ages of 5 and 10 years old who visits the store accompanied by their parents, whether or not you make a purchase. So hurry in, while the supplies last!

Bookstores should note that they can buy these books cheaper than from the publishers. Book collectors are especially invited to view our collection of hundreds of out-of-print and rare books, by and about Black folks.

So come on in and replenish your libraries—Bookstores, libraries, school teachers, parents and colleges are all welcome.

We're going to call it a day—I'm going away, I've paid my dues, now I'm buttoning up my shoes and going to some island that I'll choose.

Lewis H. Michaux

Snooze

I walk up to the bookstore today and almost fall out right there in the street. Mr. Michaux is selling all his books. He's closing down. Hell, he's being shut down . . . by the Man.

I about cry when I read his sign. . . . "This is the end of a perfect day. Farewell to my good friends of Harlem. Thank you for your support over these many years."

Class. That's Mr. Michaux in a word. Class.

If it wasn't for him, there's no way I would have finished school. I didn't do great, but I got my diploma. A *real* diploma, not just a G.E.D. Then took some business college classes. Been working down at the community center for years now. Just got another promotion. Finally got me a business card—"Samuel Walker, Youth Supervisor and Program Director."

> *I'se been a-climbin' on,*
> *And reachin' landin's,*
> *And turnin' corners . . .*
> *I'se still climbin',*

If it wasn't for that one man. . . .

I'll have to tell the kids at the center to get to the store before it closes. Mr. Michaux would like that, and it wouldn't do *them* any harm either.

SPIRIT MAGAZINE

1975

MICHAUX'S—THE MAN AND THE INSTITUTION

BY GERALD GLADNEY

He saw what time and design had done to his people. He felt the need to do
what he could to alter that state. He saw a place for himself in the world of the
printed word. Such is the beginning of what is formally known as *The National
Memorial African Bookstore*; what the owner calls "The House of Common
Sense and the Home of Proper Propaganda;" what is affectionately known
as "Michaux's."

When Dr. Lewis Michaux established his institution, the Harlem Renaissance
was waning and the Great Depression weighed heavily on the country.
The situation was anything but promising for a new black business, but Dr.
Michaux—who frankly admits that he knew nothing about the book business
when he started—established and maintained an institution that has served the
black community for nearly four decades.

At last inventory, Dr. Michaux stated he had "225,000 volumes of black books"
in his collection. These volumes included books by, about, and of importance
to black people—the works of historians, the poetry and fiction of black people,
and publications that discuss the Western religions and their roots that have
helped to shape the lives of black people—enlightening discussions that one is
not likely to come across in the churches.

But *The National Memorial African Bookstore* is more than a bookstore—which
is probably the reason it's called Michaux's. His name encompasses much
more than the word *bookstore.* The store at one time housed a Black Hall of
Fame. Michaux's contained what seemed to be an endless list of dynamic
images that ranged from the fathers of all civilization to the prophets of
this century.

Michaux's carried spoken-word recordings, photographs, art, black magazines
and was the center for many of the famous Harlem rallies. One that Dr. Michaux
recalls fondly featured keynote speaker Ghanaian President Kwame Nkrumah.

Another very important and very human aspect of the store was that one did not have to be economically endowed to enjoy the fruits of the institution. Many penniless black seekers of knowledge crossed the threshold of Michaux's and were allowed to use the store as a reference center so that those students could supplement/supplant their education/non-education.

Dr. Michaux himself is a primary source of information on contemporary history. He knew, counseled, and instructed Malcolm X, as well as others who patronized the store.

In all probability, I wouldn't be writing this article if we weren't in the process of losing Michaux's. Up until about seven years ago, Michaux's was located just off the northeast corner of Seventh Avenue and 125th Street. Then the store was forced to move closer to Lenox Avenue in order to provide space for the construction of the state office building. Now the continued construction of the state office complex is forcing Michaux's out of business, for he cannot afford another move. Vice President Rockefeller, then governor, had promised Dr. Michaux a place in the state office complex, but the subsequent change in the New York State leadership has dealt a severe blow to the fulfillment of that promise. So now we face the loss of this important black institution.

Dr. Lewis Michaux is eighty years old. He wants to retire. He has earned—with a capital 'E'—the right to retire. But the need the store spoke to still exists.

One can only hope that the Michaux magic will remain in the hearts, minds and folklore of those who touched him and were touched by him.

But the retail store, the reference center, the home of the continuous propagation of "Proper Propaganda" can be maintained. And the history of Michaux's is unimpeachable evidence for the need to maintain those elements. That much we owe ourselves, and the realization of this is the highest tribute we can pay to Dr. Lewis Michaux, the man, and the institution he created.

NORRIS E. MICHAUX III

When I first moved to the city, I would visit Uncle Lew at the bookstore when I was playing at the Apollo. Back then, I would always be with a different band—Chocolate Syrup, Slick and the Family Brick, Moment of Truth. We had many conversations in the back of his bookstore. He always encouraged me to stay with music, but not "sing the blues."

One time I visited the store I was calling myself "Jesus.'" I had really flipped. Uncle Lew said every time he sees me, I'm starting over. He asked what was wrong with having a purpose like Jesus but using my own name? Look how far I could have come, he said, if I had just been myself from the beginning. And I would still be building.

When I went back a month or so later, I was becoming MICHAUX III. At least I had come up with the concept. That's when he told me his story about the seeds. He said,

A person has to have confidence in what he's going to do. If he don't, he's not going to do it long. He has to have confidence first in his idea and next in himself.

Two men have different ideas and they go to work on them. Now the first fella's idea may come up soon. Yours may linger a long, long time, but any idea, if it's well done, will come up in its own time.

You can plant five seeds at the same moment—tomato, potato, cabbage, lettuce, beets—plant them at the same moment. And they all don't come up at the same time. If the beet would get discouraged because the cabbage come up in front of him, then there wouldn't be no beets. And if the cabbage would get discouraged because the tomato come up before his program, then there wouldn't be no cabbage.

Now the evidence of a test that's gonna come in your time of doing is the sacrifice. Hungry—that's in the making of the program. Broke—that's in the making of the program. All these things will discourage you. But you can't let them discourage you.

I believed that I would do a thing, and I went to work doin' it.

LEWIS JR.

I grew up in that store. One of my jobs on weekends was carrying the signs out in the morning. And the African flags . . . putting them in the holders near the curb.

I was only about eight or nine when Muhammad Ali came in the bookstore. I'll never forget. His hand was so big, when he shook mine, it was like a giant's. I met Malcolm X there too.

That's all over now. The store is closed. Dad was able to sell many of the books, but they went so cheap, he's taking a loss. I guess we should be thankful the state offered temporary storage for what's left.

A broken leg's bad enough, but the timing couldn't be worse. Moving the rest of the inventory will have to wait until after I get this cast off. Dad doesn't have the energy. The cancer makes it harder and harder for him to work. And Mom can't do it alone. The store would already be closed if it wasn't for her. I know we can get people to help us with the books, but we need to be at the warehouse and the store to supervise the move and keep track of the inventory.

I know Dad's glad to be retiring, but he's disappointed that the store won't be continuing. He should be proud. Because of him, many blacks were encouraged by the words they read to go out and achieve, many found pride in a heritage they never knew before, and black writers reached more readers.

I'd like to find a way to reopen the store on a small scale. Maybe offer the rare editions and some contemporary black titles. I'm not Dad and never will be. But I might be able to carry on some of his work.

Muhammad Ali and Malcolm X in Harlem

LEWIS

MARCH That old devil cancer is winning all the battles. Norris wanted to die at home, but when I saw him last week, I knew he'd never leave that hospital bed. He passed on today. I guess we all gotta go sometime, but none of us has figured out why pain has to be such a big part of the going.

Norris had his issues, but he didn't have a bad life. Sinah's a good woman and he's got three sons and some grandchildren, even great-grandchildren.

I suspect that job at the felt company wasn't his first choice, but it supported his family. And he did leave his mark on the world—the children, of course, and his "Charleston" years of dancing and shooting pool.

If I was writing his eulogy, I'd say my brother loved his family, the pool table, the beach, dancing, and even that old bullet scar. He got quite a kick out of showing it to the grandkids and telling his puffed-up version of the story.

My time's coming. What will they say about me?

FIRST ANNUAL LEWIS H. MICHAUX
BOOK FAIR FLIER
MAY 1976

On Friday and Saturday, May 21 and 22, the Studio Museum in Harlem will sponsor the First Annual Lewis H. Michaux Book Fair, in honor of one of the true legends in the world of book selling, and the institution he established and maintained for nearly four decades, the National Memorial African Bookstore. Admission is free. The event is from noon to 6:00 P.M. each day.

The book fair will include displays of books by and about blacks, and the offerings of over fifty small presses, commercial, and academic publishers. There will be an exhibition of Mr. Michaux's photographs of black literary figures and some of his rare books, manuscripts and letters. Several noted authors will participate in readings and workshops.

When the bookstore closed for good in 1975, New York lost one of its most beloved and important institutions. The book fair is not intended to reopen the bookstore, but to pay tribute to its founder, Dr. Lewis H. Michaux.

The First Annual
LEWIS H. MICHAUX
BOOK FAIR

SPONSORED BY THE STUDIO MUSEUM IN HARLEM
2033 Fifth Avenue New York, N.Y. 10035 (212) 427-5959
May 21 & 22, 1976 12 noon to 6 PM

The Book Fair is made possible by grants from the ELEANOR FRANKLIN MEMORIAL FUND OF THE NEW YORK COMMUNITY TRUST

THE NEW YORK STATE COUNCIL ON THE ARTS

NEW YORK CITY PARKS AND CULTURAL AFFAIRS ADMINISTRATION, Abraham D. Beame, *Mayor*, Patrick McGinnis, *Acting Commissioner*

POETS AND WRITERS, INC.

Admission Free

Lewis H. Michaux Book Fair poster, 1976

LEWIS

I'm not easily surprised, but the folks at Seton Hall University sure got me with that honorary doctorate. I guess I'm finally a professor . . . legitimately. I didn't need it, but it sure feels good.

The book fair, too, gave me a boost. Seeing black publishers, writers, and readers coming together. That's what's needed for black publishing to grow and survive.

They called it the "*First Annual* Lewis H. Michaux Book Fair." I'm not long for this world, but maybe the spirit of my work will live on.

NORRIS E. MICHAUX III

I've been thinking about what Uncle Lew said—when you plant your seeds, they don't all come up right away. And about the need for confidence. He told me to look back on everything I'd done and use it as a foundation to move forward.

At the hospital, I talk to Uncle Lew about a song I wrote about the seeds of our family tree. "I'm taking your knowledge and Uncle Lightfoot's knowledge and using it to create my own philosophy."

He's weak. The cancer's bad. But he manages to say, "You're building upon a strong family, a strong history that will be lost unless somebody picks it up. There has to be somebody who's a part of it in spirit to keep climbing, to make it a reality."

I leave the hospital inspired. Confident. Grateful. And sad—knowing it might be the last time I see him.

I know Uncle Lew told me not to, but tonight I might have to sing the blues.

LEWIS

AUGUST Looks like this hospital will be my last address. I remember how pitiful Lightfoot and Norris looked in their final days. Guess it's my turn.

It would be nice to have some more years. For Bettie. And our son. Suppose I should have thought of that when I was smokin' them cigarettes and working twelve-hour days at the store. I know that got old for Bettie. I could have retired sooner. Ain't nothin' I can do about it now.

Shouldn't complain though. My life was no crystal stair, far from it. But I'm taking my leave with some pride. It tickles me to know that those folks who said I could never sell books to black people are eating crow. I'd say my seeds grew pretty damn well. And not just the book business. It's the more important business of moving our people forward that has real meaning.

Lightfoot had the money, but I got something else. Where did I get that literary idea? I could have been an iceman.

When I found out about the cancer and started replaying my life, I got to wondering. So, I said, "Lord, what do you think? Did I do all right?" I got my answer about a week later.

Bettie and I were downtown in Horn and Hardart's having a cup of coffee when a young man came over and touched me on the shoulder.

"Mr. Michaux," he said, "I don't know if you remember, but my father bought me a book on medicine from you. You said I should become a doctor." He handed me his business card and said, "If you're ever in Boston, please stop in my office."

That little boy, Calvin was his name, that little boy grew up to be a doctor! I managed to stand and shake his hand. Then he hugged me like we were old friends. My eyes teared up and I knew, if I let myself, I could bawl like a baby.

Lightfoot got the money, but I'm leavin' this world a rich man. As Frederick Douglass said, it's the delight of my soul to have done something to better my race.

Snooze

AUGUST 25 When I heard Mr. Michaux died today, it sent me back to Dunbar.

> *Ah, yes, the chapter ends to-day;*
> *We even lay the book away;*
> *But oh, how sweet the moments sped*
> *Before the final page was read!*
>
> *We tried to read between the lines*
> *The Author's deep-concealed designs;*
> *But scant reward such search secures;*
> *You saw my heart and I saw yours.*

BETTIE

AUGUST 25 When you left today, I was overwhelmed with a cold feeling of loneliness. Yes, you are no longer in pain and, yes, you are in a better place. But I'm not ready—the consequences of loving an older man. Twenty-four years is not enough. People say I can "start again" at fifty-six, but who on this earth could take your place?

I'm just so mad, Lewis! Mad at you. And that damn bookstore. Good riddance. All the hours. All the years. So much of your life, of yourself you gave to that place, to its people, to everyone but *me.* You *were* the store. The store was *you.* It's what made you the man I loved. But I wish it had gone long before you.

Lewis Jr. is my comfort now. It's hard to believe he's a man. When I told him you were gone, he hugged me and said, "We'll make it, Mom." His voice was shaking, but his arms felt strong . . . safe.

Thank you for our son, my darling. Thank you for a life with purpose, a life with spirit. Thank you for our life together that was too short, but oh so very, very sweet.

Charles E. Becknell

Alex Haley said that when an older person dies, it's like a library burning to the ground. I think Haley was saying we, as African Americans, don't talk enough with our grandmothers and grandfathers and extract their life information. They take it with them when they go, and that library's gone.

Lewis Michaux took his knowledge with him. But it wasn't a complete destruction. He transferred some of it to people who came into his bookstore. He left tentacles that reached a lot of people like me. So his spirit is still here. That didn't go away with him. It's what we all need to do, leave something that spreads to other people.

LEWIS JR.

Yesterday, Dad, when you said, "You're the man of the house now," I had to swallow my tears. It wasn't the first time you'd called me a man. It was the first time I felt it was true.

You were sixty when I was born, so time was against us from the start. But you seemed to know how to make memories for me whenever we were together. And the books. The books. They're still here but, without you, when I open them, the pages seem blank.

You used to talk about the smell of books. I remember I didn't get it at first. But you taught me . . . helped me to smell the trees in the paper, the words in the ink, the history in the words . . . helped me to smell the knowing. Now, the smell of the knowing overwhelms me. And there's something else beneath it. Another smell. Your aftershave. Old Spice.

I'm shaving now. The man of the house. You treated me like a young man long before I started to shave, long before I deserved it. You didn't talk down to me like I was a child who couldn't understand.

The man of the house. Guess I have to be. Mom needs me. And I'm not so grown that I don't need her.

I may be a man, but I still need you, Dad. No one will ever fill your empty place.

> *Every day*
> *I seem to find*
> *some of you*
> *you left behind*
> *A note, a book,*
> *a rhyme or such*
> *just a trace*
> *of your personal touch*

"I LISTEN TO EVERYBODY,
BUT I DON'T *HEAR*
EVERYBODY. IT'S ALL RIGHT
TO LISTEN, BUT YOU DON'T HEAR
EVERYBODY BECAUSE IF YOU DO,
YOU CEASE TO BE YOURSELF
AND BECOME THE
FELLOW YOU HEAR.
IT'S AN INTELLIGENT THING TO
DO, TO ENTERTAIN THE MAN
WHO'S TRYING TO TELL YOU
SOMETHING, BUT NEVER
LOSE YOUR INDIVIDUALITY."

—LEWIS MICHAUX

REMEMBERING THE HARLEM PROFESSOR

James E. Turner, Cornell University

2000

As a youth, my identity was clouded by such negative images as appeared in the Tarzan movies—the pop-eyed, half-naked, savage natives. But at the National Memorial African Bookstore, I found a different reality— therapeutic and challenging as well as informative—the notion that African people are global.

The bookstore was a dramatic presence for many young Blacks, like myself, whose consciousness of the issues facing our community was just being awakened. It offered something that we were craving—a Black-centered view.

A. Peter Bailey

2001

I have my own personal collection of about twelve hundred black books. Mr. Michaux and the National Memorial African Bookstore launched me into this.

I was in my twenties in the 1960s when I was visiting the bookstore. At the time, I was too much in awe to approach Brother Michaux. He was approachable, but I was kind of wary, so I can't say I got to know him on a personal level.

I wish now that I had.

Ilyasah Shabazz, Daughter of Malcolm X and Betty Shabazz

2011

I grew up knowing of Lewis Michaux and his famous bookstore. It was the only one of its kind and attracted many scholars, historians, and students from around the country. I have a photo of my sister, Qubilah, and me on my father's lap. My father was drinking from a Chock full o'Nuts coffee mug, surrounded by mounds of books. He spent any free time he had in that store.

Lewis Michaux should be a household name for positioning this phenomenal store in Harlem. He understood the importance of history, literature, and philosophy. He made certain that great books were available to the community. It certainly helped my father and his work. I've been told Dad buried himself in there, and that he deeply respected and admired Mr. Michaux.

Books were important to my family. We had a wonderful library at home. Every Wednesday evening, we had storytelling in our living room. Books became more than stories. My parents raised us girls to know the value of reading, the importance of literature, history, accountability for self, and responsibility for others, all the while maintaining integrity— values both Dad and Mom would have encountered in Michaux's books.

Think, for example, of the trans-Atlantic slave trade—the largest forced migration of human beings ever recorded in history. Millions of technically advanced and culturally diverse Africans held in bondage that laid the foundations upon which the north, south, and central Americas as well as the Caribbean now stand. Consider the psychological trauma Africans endured for hundreds of years—stripped from their homes, land, culture, family, and friends; forbidden to read, forbidden to understand who they were as individuals and who they were as a people, forbidden to form a healthy identity, forbidden to understand the significance of history. Imagine their connectedness to the human family erased. It is inevitable that people of African ancestry would confront the challenges they face today—and that our nation and the world would be in such dire straits.

Lewis Michaux understood this, and he took action. He placed his bookstore in the center of Harlem, and the people flocked to it. They read the books he provided, and they left empowered by what they learned. They were fortified with the understanding that accurate knowledge of history prepares us for leadership in our homes. It prepares us for leadership in our communities and around the world. It enforces self-respect and then respect for others. Accurate historical knowledge led to a clear understanding that we cannot suppress another without subjugating ourselves, that we cannot come to the aid of another without helping ourselves. When we look at history, we find that even our oldest ancestors who built pyramids, erected monuments, farmed land, cattle, corn, cotton, and even danced for the rains and the sun overhead; that each gave back to society in his/her own way. When we understand such values, we understand the role each individual must play—that we are in fact our brother/sister's keeper. That each of us is responsible for one another.

The beauty and blessing of Mr. Michaux is that he assumed such a responsibility and left us with a monumental treasure.

The Reverend Dr. Charles E. Becknell Sr.

2010

As I visit places and I'm in a black community, I try to find a bookstore, but I've never seen another place like the National Memorial African Bookstore. I've never seen another place that had that focus, that energy.

When I was going to the bookstore in 1969, there was a blossoming of black literature and black awareness. I remember talking to Mr. Michaux about some of the black writers in the Harlem Renaissance. I was interested in that period because works by those artists, those writers, were beginning to resurface. They had been on bookshelves for years, but when this whole black awareness thing came about, they started coming to the forefront.

What would I read next—*Native Son? The Fire Next Time?* I remember one book Mr. Michaux recommended was *The Crisis of the Negro Intellectual.* Those were exciting times. The whole explosion of African American literature was incredible. People were hungry for it. People aren't hungry anymore.

Our history and culture is fading away. If you know the history, the foundation that our people laid, if you read, you see the sacrifice that people paid. It's about dignity. Our culture today is not being dignified. People like Mr. Michaux, and people my age, we stood for something. We had standards. What are the standards today?

Rodnell Collins,
Nephew of Malcolm X

2010

When I think of Lewis Michaux, Aaron Copland's *Fanfare for the Common Man* comes to mind. He, like Uncle Malcolm, was touchable.

Unlike many of the personalities today's young people idolize, Brother Michaux was substance. He was solid ground.

When there was going to be a rally in front of the bookstore, people would gather like it was some big rock concert. But they didn't come for entertainment. They came looking for knowledge. The educational impact of the bookstore was profound.

Poet Nikki Giovanni

2010

That bookstore was a national monument. There was no such thing as a black writer who didn't know Lewis Michaux. He was a wonderful, wonderful man.

I lived in New York for eleven years and was in the store a lot. I got to know his secretary Helen Brown fairly well too. Not personally, just the back and forth, you know.

Lewis was always very nice to me. And I had many signings at his store. It was a place that you stopped in because he knew everybody and everybody knew him. If you were looking for someone, he was the man to go to. If you wanted to know when a particular black writer was coming to town, you could ask Lewis. It was the stop-in place. If somebody was looking for *me,* Lewis could say, "Well, she stops in maybe a couple of times a week, but we can call her."

They took that whole block for the state office building. They wanted to get rid of the bookstore. You can't overlook that. There were plenty of places in Harlem they could have put that building besides 125th Street. When you look at Harlem today, you can see there were places they could have built without taking down the bookstore. They wanted to disrupt it. It's a typical story.

I think there's been a war on independent bookstores. It's a crime because books are more than just books in the African American community. Literacy and education were once the hopes for getting away from slavery, out of the ghetto, into power. Bookstores have been cultural crossroads, information centers. The bookstore is where we meet, where we talk. In the sixties, in Harlem, at 125th Street and Seventh, it was Lewis Michaux's bookstore.

Ashley Bryan,
Author and Illustrator

2010

When I went into the store, Mr. Michaux recognized me in that informal way that he had with anyone who came in. Often he was engaged with others in lively debate over contemporary or historical events affecting black life. He talked to everyone the same—the famous, the ordinary person, the intellectual.

Mr. Michaux was so close to the work. He lived there really. When you walked in, it wasn't so much the feeling of going into a store as it was a spirit of being in someone's home with things that he loved.

In the 1960s I was teaching a course on black poets at Lafayette College in eastern Pennsylvania. So I would go round the little shops in Harlem picking up on the work that was coming out of the black American poets—Sonia Sanchez, Nikki Giovanni, Gwendolyn Brooks, and a whole group of others at the time. They were coming in very small publications from Dudley Randall's Broadside Press in Detroit. Some were pamphlets, some were larger. Other small presses were also publishing the black poets. I found many of these little publications at the Michaux bookstore.

That was a time when people were out on the street expounding things about Africa, the assertion of black identity and black pride. It's the story of a people who have been put down as having no history. It was an explosion of affirming who we were and what we had given in terms of our contribution to world culture. The Michaux bookstore celebrated those contributions.

Mr. Michaux put so much of his life into his collection and the people who went to the store. The Harlem bookstore was his world, and those who have shared it count the experience as unforgettable.

A child can be reading a book and you call his name ten times, but he doesn't hear you. He's entered another world. Being in Michaux's bookstore was like that.

AUTHOR'S NOTES
ABOUT THE RESEARCH

My interest in Lewis Michaux and the National Memorial African Bookstore is both professional and personal. Lewis Michaux was my great-uncle. I visited the store only once, when I was fourteen and, regretfully, didn't realize the store's significance until years after it had closed and my uncle had passed away.

Transcripts and audio recordings of interviews with Lewis were prime resources in my research, as were family archives, articles, books, and interviews with family members and others who knew him and/or visited the store.

Researching this family history was exciting and challenging, though nonexistent and conflicting information complicated the project. I did my best to tell Lewis's story using facts where I could, filling gaps with informed speculation, making this a work of fiction. My goal was to leave readers with the essence of the man, an understanding of what shaped him, and a picture of how he and his National Memorial African Bookstore influenced a community. Most of my characters are, or were, real. In creating their voices, I used a combination of their actual words and imagined text. The few fictional characters (Snooze, Calvin, Gus Travers, and those without names) were created from the oral-history stories of real people who were touched by the bookstore. Most of the newspapers, articles, and reporters in the book are fictional but based on research. The FBI files, obtained through the Freedom of Information and Privacy Acts, appear here with minimal editing.

I've concluded that Lewis may have changed his name at some point in his life. His birth name was recorded in a family Bible as William Lonell Michaux. I knew him as Uncle Lonnie. Lewis's wife, Willie Ann, always referred to him as Lonell. It seems name changing (and not always through legal transaction) was not uncommon. Some of my father's generation added an e to Michaux, I suspect in an attempt to connect with the noted filmmaker and author Oscar Micheaux. This explains why my maiden name contains an e. (An amusing aside: Oscar's original name may have been Michaux without the e.) To avoid confusion, in my novel I spelled Norris III's last name "Michaux." In reality, his legal name was spelled Micheaux, like my own.

The bookstore's name also changed. The National Memorial Bookstore was the original name. Lewis added "African" sometime around 1960.

Lewis's true age is a bit of a mystery. According to many sources, Lewis was in his early nineties when he died, placing his year of birth at 1884 or 1885, but census reports, FBI files, and a family Bible list his birth some ten years later as August 4, October 10, or October 20, 1895. A birth certificate (in any spelling variation of Lewis Henri or William Lonell) could not be located by Virginia's Division of Vital Records. Lewis himself provides differing ages in several interviews, even in the course of a single interview. That said, it should be noted that census records and FBI files are not always accurate. For my purposes, I have used August 4, 1895, as his date of birth.

The bookstore's opening is also unclear. Various sources, including Lewis himself, give shifting start-up dates. That Lewis sold books for forty-four years is a common assertion, placing the inception at about 1931. Unable to track down a city business license, I have made an educated guess that the store began sometime in the late 1930s. My reasons include: 1) Lewis named the bookstore after his brother Lightfoot's farm project, the National Memorial to the Progress of the Colored Race in America. This undertaking wasn't conceived until 1936, when Lightfoot Michaux purchased land in Virginia. 2) The Philadelphia Church of God, where Lewis was business manager, didn't exist until 1935. It is my understanding that he married Willie Ann Tabron-Allen in 1929, and they lived in Newport News before moving to Philadelphia to help establish a branch of the Church there. If he was operating a bookstore in Harlem at this time, he would have had to commute between Philadelphia and New York or between Newport News and New York, something he alludes to in a 1970 interview. 3) FBI files give 1939 as the year the bookstore opened. 4) Lewis stated in a 1974 interview that he was at the Seventh Avenue location for twenty-eight years before having to move the store to 101 West 125th Street in 1968. This, I believe is true and would place the opening of the original store around 1939. It is important to note, however, Lewis said in the same 1974 interview, "I started this place forty years ago," suggesting the store opened in 1934. My great-uncle was quite a raconteur and not always the most reliable source.

Lewis may have first tried his hand at selling books in the early 1930s while in Philadephia. Edith Ann Foreman, the first secretary for the Church of God in Philadelphia (1935–1940), wrote in a tribute read at Lewis's funeral: "One day he walked in the office holding about five books in his hand. 'I am going to open a bookstore,' he announced. . . . 'If I can get the Negro to read, it will change his mind about life, thus changing his lifestyle. We've been told from slavery that the Negro is nothing, and he'll always be nothing. . . . I'm going to change that. I want the Negro to know and understand that he has something to contribute to society.'"

Foreman said Lewis rented a storefront, put a few books on display, and waited. He didn't sell much, but "he had caught the vision."

Lewis may have begun peddling books in Harlem without a storefront or in association with another bookseller (there are mentions of Richard B. Moore and Willis Huggins) prior to officially opening the National Memorial African Bookstore.

I was unable to document any of this. For the flow and sequence of events in my story, I have dated the bookstore's start-up at 1939.

Exactly when the business began is of little importance relative to the historic significance of Lewis Michaux and his National Memorial African Bookstore. Regardless of when the store opened, this story is worth telling and knowing.

ADDITIONAL NOTES

Lewis died before Lightfoot Michaux's estate was settled. Although the 1968 will was ultimately set aside, the estate remained unresolved for more than twenty years with legal fees exhausting most of the assets.

Lightfoot Michaux's Gospel Spreading Church of God still exists with ten churches scattered throughout Virginia, Maryland, Washington, D.C., New York, Pennsylvania, and North Carolina. *Happy News,* first published in 1933, continues its monthly circulation. In 1992, a memorial marker dedicated to Lightfoot's work was placed in Williamsburg, Virginia, near the tract of land purchased for the National Memorial to the Progress of the Colored Race in America. Currently, the land is being used for a Christian summer youth camp. Originally called the Happy Am I Summer Camp, it was renamed Camp Lightfoot following the death of the Church's founder. A dairy farm and cemetery are also on the property.

The Studio Museum in Harlem sponsored the Lewis H. Michaux Book Fair annually for six years, until 1981. As part of this event, a Lewis H. Michaux Literary Prize was awarded to a black writer. Another major book fair did not take place in Harlem until 1999, when Max Rodriguez, founder of *QBR the Black Book Review*, organized the Harlem Book Fair, an event that now draws over fifty thousand attendees and is aired on C-Span's *Book TV*.

Black bookstores in Harlem and across the United States have come and gone. San Francisco's Marcus Books (named for Marcus Garvey) opened in 1960 and may be the oldest black bookstore still operating in the country. Marcus has a second location in Oakland. Ellis' Book Store, founded by Curtis Ellis in Chicago in 1960, closed in 1985. Alfred Ligon started the Aquarian Book Shop in Los Angeles around 1940. One of the nation's largest black-owned bookstores, Aquarian closed in 1994.

Richard B. Moore sold black books door to door in Harlem in the 1930s and operated a shop in the 1940s. The Liberation Bookstore, owned by Una Mulzac, began business in 1967 on Lenox Avenue, serving the Harlem community for more than 35 years before closing its doors. Today, Harlem is home to the Hue-Man Bookstore, which Marva Allen opened in 2002 on Frederick Douglass Boulevard. Hue-Man stocks primarily black books.

With or without established storefronts, sidewalk booksellers thrive on busy Harlem streets, standing as evidence that residents still have a thirst for books and will find them wherever they can.

MICHAUX
FAMILY TREE

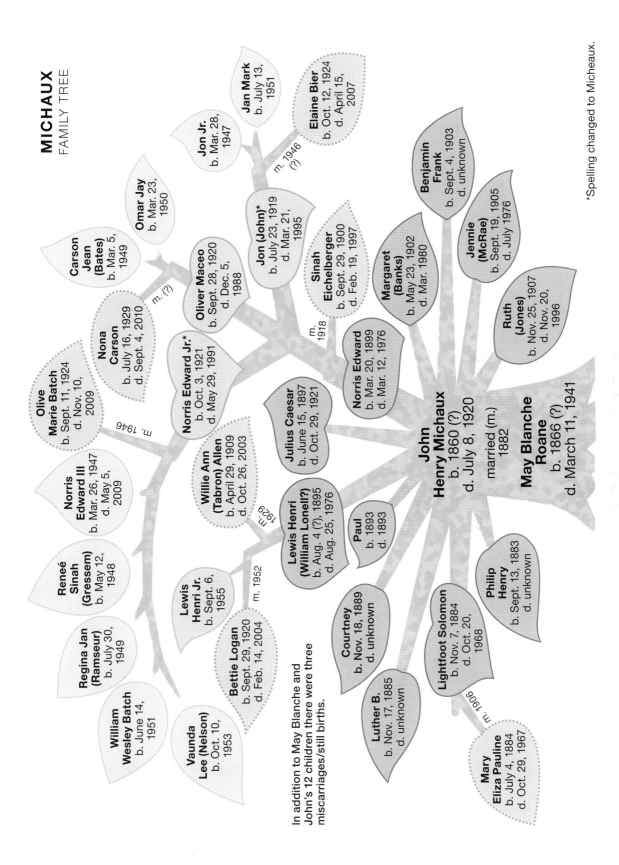

John Henry Michaux
b. 1860 (?)
d. July 8, 1920

married (m.) 1882

May Blanche Roane
b. 1866 (?)
d. March 11, 1941

In addition to May Blanche and John's 12 children there were three miscarriages/still births.

*Spelling changed to Micheaux.

Carson Jean (Bates)
b. Mar. 5, 1949

Omar Jay
b. Mar. 23, 1950

Jon Jr.
b. Mar. 28, 1947

Jan Mark
b. July 13, 1951

Elaine Bier
b. Oct. 12, 1924
d. April 15, 2007

m. 1946 (?)

Olive Marie Batch
b. Sept. 11, 1924
d. Nov. 10, 2009

Nona Carson
b. July 16, 1929
d. Sept. 4, 2010

Oliver Maceo
b. Sept. 28, 1920
d. Dec. 5, 1988

Jon (John)*
b. July 23, 1919
d. Mar. 21, 1995

Sinah Eichelberger
b. Sept. 29, 1900
d. Feb. 19, 1997

Benjamin Frank
b. Sept. 4, 1903
d. unknown

m. (?)

Norris Edward III
b. Mar. 26, 1947
d. May 5, 2009

Norris Edward Jr.*
b. Oct. 3, 1921
d. May 29, 1991

Willie Ann (Tabron) Allen
b. April 29, 1909
d. Oct. 26, 2003

Julius Caesar
b. June 15, 1897
d. Oct. 29, 1921

Margaret (Banks)
b. May 23, 1902
d. Mar. 1980

Jennie (McRae)
b. Sept. 19, 1905
d. July 1976

Norris Edward
b. Mar. 20, 1899
d. Mar. 12, 1976

m. 1918

m. 1946

Reneé Sinah (Gressem)
b. May 12, 1948

m. 1929

Lewis Henri (William Lonell?)
b. Aug. 4 (?), 1895
d. Aug. 25, 1976

Paul
b. 1893
d. 1893

Ruth (Jones)
b. Nov. 25, 1907
d. Nov. 20, 1996

Regina Jan (Ramseur)
b. July 30, 1949

Lewis Henri Jr.
b. Sept. 6, 1955

Bettie Logan
b. Sept. 29, 1920
d. Feb. 14, 2004

m. 1952

Courtney
b. Nov. 18, 1889
d. unknown

Lightfoot Solomon
b. Nov. 7, 1884
d. Oct. 20, 1968

Philip Henry
b. Sept. 13, 1883
d. unknown

William Wesley Batch
b. June 14, 1951

Vaunda Lee (Nelson)
b. Oct. 10, 1953

Luther B.
b. Nov. 17, 1885
d. unknown

m. 1906

Mary Eliza Pauline
b. July 4, 1884
d. Oct. 29, 1967

SOURCE NOTES

1   Quoted from *Third World*, "Lewis Michaux: The World's Greatest Seller of Black Books, Part 3," November, 24, 1972, 11.

3   Adapted from "Dr. Lewis Michaux," tape-recorded interview by Michele Wallace, January 18, 1974, transcript, James V. Hatch, Leo Hamalian, and Judy Blum, eds., *Artist and Influence* (New York: Hatch-Billops Collection, 1997), 123.

10   Adapted from "Louis Michaux, Owner, National Memorial Bookstore," tape-recorded interview by Robert Wright, July 31, 1970, New York City, The Civil Rights Documentation Project, Washington, DC, transcript, Moorland-Spingarn Research Center, Howard University, Washington, DC, 8–10.

11   Sentence for stealing a sack of peanuts story adapted from "Dr. Lewis Michaux," 124.

13   Adapted from "Louis Michaux, Owner, National Memorial Bookstore," 12–13.

14   "You can't walk straight . . . in a crooked system" quoted from "Louis Michaux, Owner, National Memorial Bookstore," 13.

14   Whiskey story adapted from *Encore*, "A Conversation with Lewis Michaux, Chester Himes and Nikki Giovanni," September 1972, 50.

14   "When I look at Poppa . . . staying off my knees" quoted from "Dr. Lewis Michaux," 123.

16   Marcus Garvey, quoted from Marcus Garvey Jr., "Garvey," *The McGraw-Hill Encyclopedia of World Biography* (New York: McGraw-Hill Book Co., 1973), 332.

19   "Cut box" segment and police raid story adapted from *Encore*, "A Conversation with Lewis Michaux, Chester Himes and Nikki Giovanni," 49.

21   Adapted from *Newport News (VA) Times-Herald*, October 12, 16, 1922, and Lillian Ashcraft Webb, *About My Father's Business: The Life of Elder Michaux* (Westport, CT: Greenwood Press, 1981), 22–23.

23   Exchange between Lewis and police officer adapted from *Encore*, "A Conversation with Lewis Michaux, Chester Himes and Nikki Giovanni," 49.

24   Adapted from Webb, 29.

24   "Virginia's ungodly segregation . . ." quoted from Webb, 29.

25   "Elder Lightfoot Solomon Michaux and Congregation—Happy Am I" YouTube video, posted by Madoserer, October 14, 2007, http://www.youtube.com/watch?v=DtkU5glPQ_4 (May 30, 2011).

28   "Sin sticks . . . still your record is exactly the same" adapted from *Happy News*, "Mrs. Michaux's Gospel Message to All," July 2010, 2.

28   "These people always have something up their sleeves . . . Kingdom of God," August 2002, scripture from *The King James Bible*, Titus 1:16, Psalm 101:7.

29   "These people want to go to heaven . . . satisfied with *hungry*" quoted from "Louis Michaux, Owner, National Memorial Bookstore," 2, 4.

29   "If the so-called Negro goes to school . . . take it for himself," ibid., 5, 18.

30   "The church did black folks good . . . take their minds off things here," ibid., 49.

30   "You can eat onions . . . People should be balanced in their thinking," ibid., 42.

32   "I don't want any religion . . .," Lewis H. Michaux Jr., discussion with author, 2010, scripture from *The King James Bible*, Romans 12:3, Titus 1:15.

33   Adapted from "Mrs. Michaux's Gospel Message to All," *Happy News*, August 1999, 5.

35   "I left the pulpit for the snake pit," Lewis H. Michaux Jr., discussion with author, 2010.

36–37   Quoted from Lightfoot Solomon Michaux, "Program of the National Memorial to the Progress of the Colored Race in America," presented at Golden Gate Auditorium, New York, n.d.

39   "I say so-called because . . . perpetuate slavery" quoted from "Louis Michaux, Owner, National Memorial Bookstore," 2.

39   "Seems to me if a man . . . charge for your labor" quoted from "Dr. Lewis Michaux," 125.

39   "The black man asleep . . . scratching" from *New York Times*, "Lewis Michaux, 92, Dies; Ran Bookstore in Harlem," August 27, 1976, D-15.

42   Harlem banker story adapted from *Third World*, "Lewis Michaux: The World's Greatest Seller of Black Books, Part 1," October 20, 1972, 11.

42   "If you know, you can grow," Lewis H. Michaux Jr., discussion with author, 2010.

43   "I told him I'd honor his farm project . . . who came before" adapted from "Dr. Lewis Michaux," 124, 129.

43   "Some let me comb . . . and a hundred bucks" adapted from *Encore*, "A Conversation with Lewis Michaux, Chester Himes and Nikki Giovanni," 50, and *Third World*, "Lewis Michaux: The World's Greatest Seller of Black Books, Part 1," 3.

44   Adapted from *Third World*, "Lewis Michaux: The World's Greatest Seller of Black Books, Part 2," 3.

45   "Seems he's objecting to some of the books . . . got to sell books" adapted from *Third World*, "Lewis Michaux: The World's Greatest Seller of Black Books, Part 2," 3, and "Dr. Lewis Michaux," 126.

46   Window washing story adapted from "Dr. Lewis Michaux," 125.

46   ". . . the way to hide something . . . put it in a book," Lewis H. Michaux Jr., discussion, 2010.

47   "Truth is, the whole continent . . . opportunity right here" adapted from "Louis Michaux, Owner, National Memorial Bookstore," 22–23, 38.

48   "I had but three books . . . Work gets it" quoted from "Dr. Lewis Michaux," 123–124, and *Third World*, "Lewis Michaux: The World's Greatest Seller of Black Books, Part 1," 11.

53   Adapted from Olive Batch Micheaux (former bookstore employee and niece of Lewis H. Michaux by marriage to Norris E. Micheaux Jr.), interview by author, summer 1996.

55   Adapted from *Third World*, "Lewis Michaux: The World's Greatest Seller of Black Books, Part 1," 3.

56   "Even truth carries a propaganda" quoted from *Third World*, "Lewis Michaux: The World's Greatest Seller of Black Books, Part 3," 7.

56   "I am a professor in my own field . . . he has lived a thing" quoted from "Louis Michaux, Owner, National Memorial Bookstore," 19.

57   "Garvey is a brilliant man . . . when they couldn't" quoted from *Third World*, "Lewis Michaux: The World's Greatest Seller of Black Books, Part 4," December 8, 1972, 3–4.

57   "At the time, nobody was talking . . . And he wasn't for sale" quoted from *Encore*, "A Conversation with Lewis Michaux, Chester Himes and Nikki Giovanni," 47–49.

58   Quotes from Elder Lightfoot Solomon Michaux, *Sparks from the Anvil of Elder Michaux*, comp., ed. Pauline Lark (New York: Vantage Press, 1950), 16, 53, 86, 21, 139.

60   "You can be black as a crow . . . that's fo' sho'" quoted from *Third World*, "Lewis Michaux: The World's Greatest Seller of Black Books, Part 1," 3.

60   Calvin story adapted from *Third World*, "Lewis Michaux: The World's Greatest Seller of Black Books, Part 1," 3, and "Dr. Lewis Michaux," 127.

62–63   Calvin story adapted from ibid.

66-67   Langston Hughes, *The Dream Keeper and Other Poems* (New York: Alfred A. Knopf, 1993), 2, 64.

69-70   Poetry from ibid., 63, and Paul Laurence Dunbar, *The Complete Poems of Paul Laurence Dunbar* (New York: Dodd, Mead & Company, 1944), 9–10.

71   Story adapted from "Dr. Lewis Michaux," 126.

76   Adapted from "Louis Michaux, Owner, National Memorial Bookstore," 6, 20, 35; *Third World,* "Lewis Michaux: The World's Greatest Seller of Black Books, Part 5," December 22, 1972, 3; *Encore*, "A Conversation with Lewis Michaux, Chester Himes and Nikki Giovanni," 48, 49; *Third World*, "Lewis Michaux: The World's Greatest Seller of Black Books, Part 4," 3, 13; Peter Goldman, *The Death and Life of Malcolm X*, 2nd ed. (Urbana: University of Illinois Press, 1979), 52.

78   Adapted from Hugh Pearson, *When Harlem Nearly Killed King* (New York: Seven Stories Press, 2002), 39–45, 65–68; David Garrow, *Bearing the Cross: Martin Luther King, Jr., and the Southern Christian Leadership Conference* (New York: William Morrow & Co., 1986), 109–112; Stephen B. Oates, *Let the Trumpet Sound: A Life of Martin Luther King, Jr.* (New York: Harper Perennial, 1994), 137–140.

80   Adapted from *Third World,* "Lewis Michaux: The World's Greatest Seller of Black Books, Part 4," 13.

82   Adapted from *Encore*, "A Conversation with Lewis Michaux, Chester Himes and Nikki Giovanni," 49, and *Third World*, "Lewis Michaux: The World's Greatest Seller of Black Books, Part 5," 12.

87-88   Goddam White Man story adapted from *Encore*, "A Conversation with Lewis Michaux, Chester Himes and Nikki Giovanni," 46, and *Third World*, "Lewis Michaux: The World's Greatest Seller of Black Books, Part 3," 7.

88   "If I wake up . . . trouble's got to happen" quoted from "Louis Michaux, Owner, National Memorial Bookstore," 14.

89   James E. Turner (founding director of the Africana Studies and Research Center at Cornell University), telephone interview with author, November 6, 2000.

89   From *Encore*, "A Conversation with Lewis Michaux, Chester Himes and Nikki Giovanni," 49.

91-92   Adapted from *New York Amsterdam News*, "9000 Hear Muhammad in Capital," September 16, 1961, 23; *Jet*, "Over 4,000 Hear Michaux, Muhammad Religious Debate," September 28, 1961, 21; and Louis A. DeCaro Jr., *Malcolm and the Cross: The Nation of Islam, Malcolm X, and Christianity* (New York: New York University Press, 1998), 144–145.

94   "Everyone has ears to hear, but not everyone can hear God" quoted from *Happy News*, "Mrs. Michaux's Gospel Message to All," March 2009, 2, scripture from *The King James Bible*, St. Matthew 11:15.

96   A. Peter Bailey (journalist and former bookstore patron), taped telephone interview with author, March 19, 2001, and follow-up telephone discussions, 2001–2011.

99   Coffee story adapted from *Encore*, "A Conversation with Lewis Michaux, Chester Himes and Nikki Giovanni," 48, and "Dr. Lewis Michaux," 125.

101   Malcolm X comment at rally adapted from *New York Times*, "Malcolm X Scores U.S. and Kennedy," December 2, 1963, 21.

102   Adapted from *Third World*, "Lewis Michaux: The World's Greatest Seller of Black Books, Part 5," 3.

103   Adapted from *Encore*, "A Conversation with Lewis Michaux, Chester Himes and Nikki Giovanni," 48; "Louis Michaux, Owner, National Memorial Bookstore," 34; *Third World*, "Lewis Michaux: The World's Greatest Seller of Black Books, Part 5," 3.

105	"He was a major influence . . . impressed by his oratorical skills" quoted from Rodnell P. Collins, *Seventh Child: A Family Memoir of Malcolm X*, with A. Peter Bailey (Secaucus, NJ: Carol Publishing Group, 1998), 94.
105	Abdullah Abdur-Razzaaq, former social secretary for Malcolm X, telephone conversation with author, March 7, 2011.
106	Bailey interview and discussions.
107	"I was to be on the platform . . . sitting beside him" adapted from "Dr. Lewis Michaux," 129, and *Third World*, "Lewis Michaux: The World's Greatest Seller of Black Books, Part 5," 3.
111	Lewis H. Michaux Jr., discussion with author, 2011.
111	Lewis H. Michaux Jr., discussion with author, 2010, and Goldman, 377.
111	"They had to get rid . . . freest man" quoted from *Encore*, "A Conversation with Lewis Michaux, Chester Himes and Nikki Giovanni," 47.
111	"The Nation of Islam . . . spellbound" adapted from "Louis Michaux, Owner, National Memorial Bookstore," 35.
111–112	"Malcolm is reincarnated . . . Let it come!" quoted from *Third World*, "Lewis Michaux: The World's Greatest Seller of Black Books, Part 2," 13.
112	Bailey interview.
113	Adapted from Collins and Bailey, *Seventh Child,* 93–94, 191.
114	Adapted from *Third World*, "Lewis Michaux: The World's Greatest Seller of Black Books, Part 4," 13.
117	". . . have been throwing . . . you're responsible" adapted from *Third World*, "Lewis Michaux: The World's Greatest Seller of Black Books, Part 3," 7.
117	"Some men came to me . . . as an individual," ibid, 11.
118	Adapted from "Dr. Lewis Michaux," 126–127, and Lewis H. Michaux Jr., discussion with author, 2010.
118	Adapted from "Dr. Lewis Michaux," 128–129.
119	"I didn't make enough money . . . nine years old" adapted from *Third World*, "Lewis Michaux: The World's Greatest Seller of Black Books, Part 1," 3, 11.
119	"Every company that publishes . . . built up my reputation" adapted from "Dr. Lewis Michaux," 125–126.
119	"If you can't find it . . . sincere in what you're doing" quoted from *Encore*, "A Conversation with Lewis Michaux, Chester Himes and Nikki Giovanni," 47.
119	"True, I haven't been to a show . . . back to get that baby" quoted from *Third World*, "Lewis Michaux: The World's Greatest Seller of Black Books, Part 1," 11.
119	"Sure I could move . . . out of here for nothing" quoted from *Third World*, "Lewis Michaux: The World's Greatest Seller of Black Books, Part 3," 11.

121   Adapted from *Third World*, "Lewis Michaux: The World's Greatest Seller of Black Books, Part 3," 11–12.

123   Nikki Giovanni (poet and former bookstore patron), taped telephone interview by the author, May 31, 2010.

124   Adapted from *Third World*, "Lewis Michaux: The World's Greatest Seller of Black Books, Part 2," 3.

126   Giovanni telephone interview.

126   Lewis H. Michaux Jr. (son of Lewis H. Michaux), tape-recorded interview by the author, August 1999, and follow-up discussions via phone and e-mail, 1999–2011.

127   "Violence originated in Heaven . . . when he's attacked" quoted from *Third World*, "Lewis Michaux: The World's Greatest Seller of Black Books, Part 2," 13.

127   "Until the neglected . . . nowhere!" Lewis H. Michaux Jr., discussion, 2010.

127   "Only a tree . . . chopped down" from Gerald C. Fraser, "Lewis Michaux Is Eulogized in Harlem as a Bookseller Who Changed Lives," *New York Times*, August 31, 1976, 31.

130   Adapted from "Dr. Lewis Michaux," 127–128, and "Louis Michaux, Owner, National Memorial Bookstore," 40.

132   "Was there a political agenda . . . any lengths to stifle them?" from Basir Mchawi, "Another Kind of Warrior," *Black News*, October 1976, 10–11.

133   Adapted from Chuck Moore, *I Was a Black Panther* (New York: Doubleday and Company, 1970), 33–40.

140   Charles E. Becknell Sr. (pastor and former bookstore patron), taped interview with author, June 18, 2010.

142   "Since the Rock left office . . . east side of the state office building" adapted from "Dr. Lewis Michaux," 128.

142   "We understood there was no room . . . silent on the matter" adapted from ibid.

144   *Jet Magazine*, "Eviction of Harlem Bookstore Owner Is Protested By Leaders," February 7, 1974, 28–29.

146   "Nature produces you and nature . . . want to die on the battlefield," Lewis H. Michaux Jr., discussion.

147   Adapted from *New York Amsterdam News*, advertisement, October 26, 1974.

149–150 Adapted from Gerald Gladney, "Michaux's—The Man and the Institution," *Spirit Magazine: An African Publication*, Spring 1975, 28–29.

151–152 Adapted from taped conversation between Lewis Michaux and his great-nephew Norris E. Micheaux III, and discussions with Norris E. Micheaux III. "A person has to have confidence . . . went to work doin' it" quoted from ibid.

152   Lewis H. Michaux Jr. (son of Lewis H. Michaux), tape-recorded interview by the author, August 1999, and follow-up discussions via phone and e-mail, 1999–2011.

154   *New York Daily Challenge*, "The First Annual Michaux Book Fair," April 6, 1976, 9.

155   "You're building upon . . . make it a reality" from taped conversation, between Lewis Michaux and Micheaux III, and Micheaux III, discussions.

156   "Where did I get this literary idea? . . . iceman" from "Dr. Lewis Michaux," 125.

156   Calvin/doctor story adapted from *Third World*, "Lewis Michaux: The World's Greatest Seller of Black Books, Part 1," 3.

157   Becknell interview.

158   Adapted from a poem by Norris E. Micheaux Jr.

159   "I listen to everybody . . . lose your individuality" from "Louis Michaux, Owner, National Memorial Bookstore," 6, 18.

PERMISSIONS

BIBLIOGRAPHY

Alexander, J. B. "Black Culture Was His Cause." *New York Post*, May 21, 1976, 9.

Alternatives. "Louis Michaux—Guardian of the Black Archives." April 1974, 6, 8.

Anderson, Jervis. *This Was Harlem: A Cultural Portrait, 1900–1950*. New York: Farrar, Straus and Giroux, 1982.

Angelou, Maya. *The Heart of a Woman*. New York: Bantam Books, 1997.

Barker, Kevin. "Seeking Malcolm." *American Legacy: The Magazine of African American History and Culture*, Fall 2006, 16–26.

Betserai, Tarabu. "Lewis and Elder," character study with letter to Norris E. Micheaux III, December 12, 1989. Unpublished.

Blockson, Charles L. *"Damn Rare": The Memoirs of an African-American Bibliophile*. Tracy, CA: Quantum Leap Publisher, 1998.

Cobb, Charles E., Jr. "ZipUSA: Harlem, New York." *National Geographic*, April 2001, 120–124.

Collins, Rodnell P. *Seventh Child: A Family Memoir of Malcolm X*. With A. Peter Bailey. Secaucus, NJ: Carol Publishing Group, 1998.

Cronon, E. David. "Garvey, Marcus (Mosiah)." *Dictionary of American Negro Biography*. New York: W. W. Norton & Company, 1982, 254.

DeCaro, Louis A., Jr. *Malcolm and the Cross: The Nation of Islam, Malcolm X, and Christianity*. New York: New York University Press, 1998.

Douglass, Frederick. *Narrative of the Life of Frederick Douglass, an American Slave, Written by Himself (1845)*. Boston: Bedford/St. Martin's, 1993.

Dunbar, Paul Laurence. *The Complete Poems of Paul Laurence Dunbar*. New York: Dodd, Mead & Company, 1944.

Dyer, Coleen, and Michelle M. Kenyon. "The Heart of Harlem." *Country Home*, February 1995, 26–30, 121.

Emblidge, David. "Rallying Point: Lewis Michaux's National Memorial African Bookstore." *Publishing Research Quarterly* 24, no. 4, December 2008, 267–276.

Encore. "A Conversation with Lewis Michaux, Chester Himes and Nikki Giovanni." September 1972, 46–51.

Federal Bureau of Investigation. Subject: Michaux, Lewis Henry. Freedom of Information and Privacy Acts, 1959–1968.

Fraser, C. Gerald. "Lewis Michaux, 92, Dies; Ran Bookstore in Harlem." *New York Times*, August 27, 1976, D-15.

——. "Lewis Michaux Is Eulogized in Harlem as a Bookseller Who Changed Lives." *New York Times*, August 31, 1976, 31.

——. "Lewis H. Michaux—One for the Books." *New York Times*, May 23, 1976, 55.

Garrow, David J. *Bearing the Cross: Martin Luther King Jr, and the Southern Christian Leadership Conference.* New York: William Morrow and Co., 1986.

Garvey, Marcus, Jr. "Garvey." *The McGraw-Hill Encyclopedia of World Biography*. New York: McGraw-Hill Book Co., 1973, 331–332.

Gladney, Gerald. "Michaux's—The Man and the Institution," *Spirit Magazine: An African Publication*, Spring 1975, 28–29.

Goldman, Peter. *The Death and Life of Malcolm X*. 2nd ed. Urbana: University of Illinois Press, 1979.

Green, Cheryll Y. "A Book Fair in Harlem." *Freedomways*, Second Quarter, 1976, 112.

Hamilton, Willie L. "Louis Michaux, a Familiar Face." *New York Amsterdam News*, January 19, 1974, A-4.

Harris, Janette Hoston. "Michaux, Elder Solomon Lightfoot." *Dictionary of American Negro Biography*. New York: W. W. Norton & Company, 1982, 432.

The Holy Bible: The Authorized King James Version. Cleveland: World Publishing Company, n.d.

Hughes, Langston. *The Dream Keeper and Other Poems*. New York: Alfred A. Knopf, 1993.

Hunter, Charlayne. "The Professor." *New Yorker*, September 3, 1966, 28–29.

Jackson, David. "An Intimate History of the Lewis H. Michaux Book Fair (1976–1979)." Publisher's information unavailable.

Jet. "Eviction of Harlem Bookstore Owner Is Protested by Leaders." February 7, 1974, 28–29.

Johnson, Samuel M. *Often Back: Tales of Harlem*. New York: Vantage Press, 1971.

Lopez, Sharon Y. "Up in Harlem." *Crisis*, October 1981, 20–21.

Malcolm X. *The Autobiography of Malcolm X*. With Alex Haley. New York: Ballantine Books, 1992. First published 1965 by Grove Press.

The Man and His Vision: Elder Lightfoot Solomon Michaux, Celebrating 85 Years of Grace, 1919–2004. Gospel Spreading Church of God, 2004.

Meltzer, Milton. *Langston Hughes: An Illustrated Edition*. Brookfield, CT: Millbrook Press, 1997.

Michaux, Lewis. "Dr. Lewis Michaux." Taped interview by Michele Wallace, January 18, 1974. Transcript, James V. Hatch, Leo Hamalian, and Judy Blum, eds. *Artist and Influence*. New York: Hatch-Billops Collection, 1997, 120–129.

——. "Louis Michaux, Owner, National Memorial Bookstore." Taped interview by Robert Wright, July 31, 1970, New York City. The Civil Rights Documentation Project, Washington, DC. Transcript, Moorland-Spingarn Research Center, Howard University, Washington, DC.

——. "Special SALE Notice: The People of Harlem from the National Memorial African Bookstore," *New York Amsterdam News* advertisement, October 26, 1974.

Michaux, Lightfoot Solomon. "Program of the National Memorial to the Progress of the Colored Race in America," presented at Golden Gate Auditorium, New York, NY, n.d.

———. *Sparks from the Anvil of Elder Michaux*. Compiled and edited by Pauline Lark. New York: Vantage Press, 1950.

Micheaux, Norris E., III, and Lewis Michaux. Taped conversation between Lewis Michaux and his great-nephew, Norris E. Micheaux, III, Flowers 5th Avenue Hospital, New York, 1976.

Moore, Chuck. *I Was a Black Panther*. New York: Doubleday and Company, 1970.

New York Amsterdam News. "Michaux Fights for Bookstore." Februrary 9, 1974, B3.

New York Daily Challenge. "Annual Michaux Book Fair." May 17, 1978, 7.

New York Daily Challenge. "The First Annual Michaux Book Fair." April 6, 1976, 9.

New York Post. "Obituaries: Lewis Michaux, 92." August 27, 1976, 48.

New York Times. "Malcolm X Scores U.S. and Kennedy." December 2, 1963, 21.

Oates, Stephen B. *Let the Trumpet Sound: A Life of Martin Luther King, Jr.* New York: Harper Perennial, 1994.

Pearson, Hugh. *When Harlem Nearly Killed King: The 1958 Stabbing of Martin Luther King, Jr.* New York: Seven Stories Press, 2002.

"Presenting a Pictorial Review of Elder Lightfoot Solomon Michaux, International Radio Evangelist." Gospel Spreading Church of God, n.d.

"A Sketch of the Life of Elder Lightfoot Solomon Michaux." Gospel Spreading Church of God. n.d.

Tapley, Mel. "Lewis Michaux Buried—4 Decades of Service." *New York Amsterdam News*, September 4, 1976, C-14.

Third World. "Lewis Michaux: The World's Greatest Seller of Black Books, Part 1." October 20, 1972, 1, 3, 11.

———. "Lewis Michaux: The World's Greatest Seller of Black Books, Part 2." November 2, 1972, 3, 13.

———. "Lewis Michaux: The World's Greatest Seller of Black Books, Part 3." November 24, 1972, 7, 11–12.

———. "Lewis Michaux: The World's Greatest Seller of Black Books, Part 4." December 8, 1972, 3, 4, 13.

———. "Lewis Michaux: The World's Greatest Seller of Black Books, Part 5." December 22, 1972, 3, 12.

Thomas, Lorenzo. "Garvey, Marcus Moziah." *The African American Encyclopedia*. New York: Marshall Cavendish, 1993, 644.

Webb, Lillian Ashcraft. *About My Father's Business: The Life of Elder Michaux*. Westport, CT: Greenwood Press, 1981.

Wilson, Sondra Kathryn. *Meet Me at the Theresa*. New York: Simon & Schuster, 2004.

INTERVIEWS

Bailey, A. Peter (journalist and former bookstore patron). Taped telephone interview with author, March 19, 2001, and follow-up telephone discussions 2001–2011.

Becknell, Charles E., Sr. (pastor, Emmanuel Missionary Baptist Church, and former bookstore patron). Taped interview with author, June 18, 2010.

Bryan, Ashley (artist-author and former bookstore patron). Taped telephone interview by the author, September 13, 2010.

Collins, Rodnell (author, son of Kenneth and Ella Collins [Malcolm X's sister], nephew of Malcolm X). Telephone interview with the author, March 2001, and follow-up telephone discussions, 2010–2011.

Giovanni, Nikki (poet and former bookstore patron). Taped telephone interview with the author, May 31, 2010.

Hurst, Anthony (former assistant pastor, Church of God in New York City, and former associate minister, Church of God Philadephia). Telephone conversation, December 13, 2000, and follow-up discussions via e-mail and telephone with the author, 2000–2011.

Jackson, David Earl (program coordinator for the Lewis H. Michaux Book Fair, 1976–1979), telephone interview with the author, February 2001.

Michaux, Lewis. Tape-recorded interview by Gil Noble, "Like It Is," WABC-TV, December 8, 1974.

Michaux, Lewis H., Jr. (son of Lewis H. Michaux). Taped interview with the author, August 1999, and follow-up discussions via telephone and e-mail, 1999–2011.

Micheaux, Olive Batch (former bookstore employee and niece of Lewis H. Michaux by marriage to Norris E. Micheaux Jr.). Interview with the author, summer 1996.

Robinson, Willie (chairman of the board of deacons for the New York Church of God). Telephone interview with the author, December 26, 2000.

Shabazz, Ilyasah (daughter of Malcolm X). Taped telephone interview with the author, March 7, 2011.

Turner, James E. (founding director of the Africana Studies and Research Center at Cornell University). Telephone interview with the author, November 6, 2000.

FURTHER READING

Benson, Michael. *Malcolm X*. Minneapolis: Lerner Publications Company, 2001.

Bloom, Harold. *The Harlem Renaissance*. New York: Chelsea House Publications, 2004.

Giovanni, Nikki. *Shimmy Shimmy Shimmy Like My Sister Kate: Looking at the Harlem Renaissance Through Poems*. New York: Henry Holt, 1996.

Hardy, Sheila, and P. Stephen Hardy. *Extraordinary People of the Civil Rights Movement*. New York: Scholastic, 2007.

Helfer, Andrew, ed. *Malcolm X: A Graphic Biography*. New York: Hill and Wang, 2006.

Hill, Laban Carrick. *Harlem Stomp!: A Cultural History of the Harlem Renaissance*. New York: Little, Brown and Company, 2009.

Kallen, Stuart A. *Marcus Garvey and the Back to Africa Movement*. San Diego: Lucent Books, 2006.

Leach, Laurie F. *Langston Hughes: A Biography*. Westport, CT: Greenwood Press, 2004.

Meltzer, Milton. *Langston Hughes: An Illustrated Edition*. Minneapolis: Millbrook Press, 1997.

Myers, Walter Dean. *Here in Harlem: Poems in Many Voices*. New York: Holiday House, 2004.

ACKNOWLEDGMENTS

There is a large cast of people, some of whom have passed on, who played parts, large and small, in this project of more than 15 years. I owe much to family, longtime and newfound friends, librarians, fellow writers, editors, and those who gave their time and shared their knowledge of, and affection for, Lewis Michaux and his National Memorial African Bookstore.

I am deeply indebted to my cousin, Lewis Henri Michaux Jr., who generously entrusted me with his father's story and, during my research trips, shared so much of himself and Lewis's life with me, as well as taught me how to navigate the New York City subway system. For their stories, photographs, scrapbooks, and love, I thank my grandmother Sinah Eichelberger Michaux; my mother and father, Olive Batch Micheaux and Norris E. Micheaux Jr.; and my brother, Norris E. Micheaux III, all of whom I know are looking down from Heaven and I hope with pride. I owe much to my sisters, Renee Sinah Gressem and Regina Jan Ramseur, and brother William Wesley Batch Micheaux, for photographs, genealogical brainstorming, and unconditional support. Thanks, also, to the late Willie Ann Michaux-Edwards, and to my cousins Jon Micheaux Jr., Jan Micheaux, and Carson Jean Bates. A heap of hugs for all my family who have cheered me on through this challenging project.

Unending thanks to the amazing women in my writing critique group who have lived with this project for many years, read and reread numerous drafts and revisions— Katherine Hauth, Stephanie Farrow, Uma Krishnaswami, and the late Lucy Hampson— the stones upon which this story was polished.

Special thanks to Kathy Dawson, who provided guidance and extensive comments when the manuscript was in its earliest form back in 2001. My gratitude to Jeanne Whitehouse, Kate Harrington, Rob Spiegel, Penelope Stowell, Lynne Polvino, and Stephanie Zaslav for their helpful feedback.

I was blessed to connect with current and past members of the Gospel Spreading Church of God including Deacon Jasper W. Sturdivant (Washington, D.C., Church of God), Deacon Willie Robinson (New York Church of God), and Donald Harris and Theresa Edwards (Newport News Church of God), who all welcomed me with kindness and provided invaluable historical resources. Extra special thanks to former Church of God member Anthony Hurst for his generous contributions to the book and his kind friendship.

Thanks to the Society of Children's Book Writers and Illustrators for selecting me as the recipient of an SCBWI/Anna Cross Giblin Work-in-Progress grant, which made some of my research possible. And to SCBWI New Mexico for ongoing support.

I am truly grateful to Joseph McKenzie, interlibrary loan librarian at Rio Rancho Public Library, and Auburn Nelson, Senior Reference Librarian at the Schomburg

Center for Research and Black Culture, for often going that extra mile, or ten, to locate a resource. And also to Joellen ElBashir of Howard University's Moorland-Spingarn Research Center, James V. Hatch of the Hatch-Billops Collection, Elizabeth Brown of The Studio Museum in Harlem, and to Newport News Public Library, Library of Virginia, and professional researcher Anne Taylor Brown. All provided valuable assistance.

Thank you Marilyn Schroeder, Kimberly McCrae Miller, Toni Beatty, Christyl and Justin and the Browns, Betsy White, Lori and Greg and the Snyders, Rob Nankin, William Cicola, and my friends and colleagues at Rio Rancho Public Library for your enduring support.

For their fine contributions, I am obliged to Ida Lewis, Nikki Giovanni, A. Peter Bailey, Rodnell Collins, Professor James E. Turner, the Reverend Dr. Charles E. Becknell Sr., Ilyasah Shabazz, Abdullah Abdur-Razaaq, Marie Brown, and the late David Earl Jackson. Additional thanks to Don Fox, John Farrow, David Emblidge, Sherry Sherrod DuPree, Louis A. DeCaro Jr., Marva Allen, Max Rodriguez, and Tarabu Betserai.

I am especially honored by the contribution, support and friendship of Ashley Bryan. I am grateful, too, for the thoughtfulness of Walter Dean Myers.

A thousand thanks to Tracey and Josh Adams of Adams Literary for the gift of time; they are always behind the scenes taking care of business so that I can write.

Many, many thanks to my outside-the-box editor Andrew Karre for his belief and delight in Lewis's story; and to the wonderful staff at Lerner Publishing Group—Adam Lerner, Mary Rodgers, Julie Harman, Danielle Carnito, Zach Marell, Elizabeth Dingmann, Erica Johnson, Sarah Marquart, Lindsay Matvick, Terri Lynn Soutor, Lois Wallentine, Kathleen Clarke, and Brad Richason.

And to R. Gregory Christie for his stylistic interpretation of Lewis's world.

I'm most beholden to my husband, Drew, my first editor and best friend. His love and patience are beyond measure. This book would not have happened without him. Thank you, my darling.

To all who have escaped mention, please forgive me, and know that I appreciate your contributions.

Above all, I thank my Lord for enabling me to fulfill this dream.

INDEX OF HISTORICAL CHARACTERS

PHOTO ACKNOWLEDGMENTS

The images in this book are used with the permission of: Schomburg Center for Research in Black Culture, Photographs and Prints Division, The New York Public Library, Astor, Lenox and Tilden Foundations, p. 14; The Marcus Garvey and UNIA Papers Project, African Studies Center, UCLA, p. 15; Courtesy of Anthony W. Hurst Sr., p. 26; © J. R. Eyerman/Time & Life Pictures/Getty Images, p. 30; Gospel Spreading Church of God, Courtesy of Vaunda Micheaux Nelson, pp. 40, 45; Courtesy of the John W. Mosley Photographic Collection, Charles L. Blockson Afro-American Collection, Temple University Libraries, Philadelphia, Pennsylvania, p. 44; Courtesy of Vaunda Micheaux Nelson, pp. 49, 51 (both), 52, 53, 71, 115, 122, 136, 139, 145 (both), 154; Schomburg Center for Research in Black Culture, General Research and Reference Division, The New York Public Library, Astor, Lenox and Tilden Foundations, p. 63; The Kansas Collection, Kenneth Spencer Research Library, University of Kansas Libraries, p. 66; © Time & Life Pictures/Getty Images, p. 75; AP Photo/John Lent, p. 78; © Bettmann/ CORBIS, pp. 82, 101, 105, 114; © Henri Cartier-Bresson/Magnum Photos, p. 88; © Marvin Lichtner/Time & Life Pictures/Getty Images, p. 96; © Ted Russell/Time & Life Pictures/Getty Images, p. 99; AP Photo/WCBS-TV, p. 110; Library of Congress, p. 118 (LC-DIG-ppmsca-11683); Nikki Giovanni, Courtesy of Vaunda Micheaux Nelson, p. 123; AP Photo, p. 124; © Ezio Peterson, Courtesy of Vaunda Micheaux Nelson, p. 140; © John Peodincuk/NY Daily News Archive/Getty Images, p. 152; © Laura Westlund/Independent Picture Service, p. 169.

ABOUT THE AUTHOR

Vaunda Micheaux Nelson is the author of many books for young readers, including *Bad News for Outlaws: The Remarkable Life of Bass Reeves, Deputy U.S. Marshal*, which won the Coretta Scott King Award in 2010, and *Almost to Freedom*, which won a Coretta Scott King Honor for Colin Bootman's illustrations in 2004. Nelson is a youth services librarian at the public library in Rio Rancho, New Mexico, where she lives with her husband.

To write *No Crystal Stair*, she spent years researching Lewis Michaux's life. She conducted interviews, sifted through library collections, examined family archives, and interviewed those who knew Michaux. In the end though, the man's full story (and even his date of birth) remained elusive. Only the tools of fiction could make a complete portrait.

ABOUT THE ILLUSTRATOR

R. Gregory Christie's illustrations have earned him three Coretta Scott King Honors and two spots on the *New York Times*' annual Best Illustrated Children's Books lists. He has also illustrated numerous jazz album covers and is a regular contributor to the *New Yorker* magazine.